MW01248004

DISASTERPIECES

WESLEY SOUTHARD & WILE E. YOUNG

SOUTH OF HEAVEN PRESS
York, Pennsylvania

Cover Art by Justicia Satria

Cover & Interior Layout by Scott Cole
(www.13visions.com)

ALSO FROM WESLEY SOUTHARD

For Stephen Kozeniewski
You don't win friends with salad…

EVERYBODY WANTS TO RULE THE WORLD

WESLEY SOUTHARD

RIVERS OF MERCY

WILE E. YOUNG

EVERYBODY WANTS TO RULE THE WORLD

WESLEY SOUTHARD

The rumble was first, then the explosion.

There was no time for Miguel Toro to react. The thunder above all their heads was a brief grumble, like the throaty build-up to a lion's growl, and when the roar came, it was deafening and bright. The ceiling detonated, a fiery eruption that rocked everyone right out of their cubical chairs. Like the explosion itself, screams immediately pervaded their open work area. A snarl of fire ripped through the tight office space, racing across the ceiling and down the walls. Another explosion rocked the room. More fire cascaded onto the floor, running like a sprung faucet. Hordes of tile and ductwork dropped loose and crashed to the floor. In a flash, something heavy fell onto Miguel's midsection, driving the air from his lungs, pinning him to the floor. More screams filled the room—many cries abruptly cut short.

On his back, Miguel sucked in shallow breaths and howled in pain. He was unable to move. His ears rang, his nostrils filling with acrid smoke. Through the din, a woman somewhere close gurgled a wet scream. Miguel tried to call for her, tried to push the bulky debris from his body, but lightheadedness promptly washed over him, threatening to swallow him whole. The woman's screams grew desperate. Despite his own agony, he wished he could help.

The world suddenly went quiet, as if taking its last deep breath. Miguel craned his head upward. When the world exhaled with another explosion, the hellscape above came down to greet him.

It could have been minutes, hours, or even days by the time Miguel came to. He awoke with a start, sucking in a deep, desperate breath before gagging and coughing. Only one eye was able to fully open, as his other was swollen shut. His skull resonated with a terrible song, and a surge of nausea swept over him, causing him to panic. It only took a moment to remember he couldn't move. His chest and lower body were still pinned down by a large section of metal air conditioning ductwork, and now his right arm was being held captive by a long, thick length of rebar. The skin underneath had been broken open, blood weeping from the gaping wound. Luckily, Miguel couldn't feel it at all. The bar, he realized, must have come loose in the second explosion and knocked him out, then hit his arm, tearing it open before settling in place. His appendage was completely numb. He willed his fingers to flex, to even flinch, but they wouldn't move.

Above his head, the ceiling was mostly gone. Save for a few spots of tile and concrete still clinging to the crossbeams, the majority of the area above them in the building had been blown away, completely opening up the floor above them. Even the ceiling above that was gone, and through the thick haze of gray smoke, Miguel could almost see three floors above that. Though he couldn't see much to his sides from the debris, somehow the floor beneath his back remained intact.

The blaze continued to feed, devouring the room around him.

"Oh, God!" he groaned helplessly. "I don't want to die."

A frightened shriek echoed behind him.

Startled, Miguel flinched. "*Hello?*" He tried to lift his head, but nausea and vertigo prevented him from doing so. He coughed and swallowed, attempting to wet his mouth. "Hello?"

The same voice had now become a pitiful scream that carried on like a wet gurgle. The woman sucked in a breath, then continued to cry out again, her vocal cords heavy with strain.

Locating the voice, Miguel carefully lifted his head backwards to see behind him.

In the glow of the flames, he spotted his co-worker Camille behind a row of overturned desks. She was an older white woman, lost somewhere in her fifties, long red hair that nearly reached her rear end, and skin so pale, Miguel always joked, he could see the person behind her. Despite being married with three children, she had a tendency to be the office tease, flirting with little male discrimination, no matter who they were. Miguel supposed it was her way of passing the time, the monotony of three decades of desk work doldrums needing to be broken. Miguel didn't mind. He imagined none of his married male co-workers minded much. He was positive she would not have actually acted on it, which made reciprocal touches and words all the more innocent.

From what Miguel could see, Camille wasn't going to be active in flirting much anymore. A large mixture of ceiling rubble had nearly crushed her. While one of her arms was underneath an overturned cabinet, the other had been severed at the elbow. The remainder of her lower left arm was sitting only a few feet from Miguel's head. The burgundy painted nails of her fingers were curled inward toward her palm, looking more like a gnarled tree limb than a human arm. Blood spat from the ragged hole in her arm, spraying up onto her body and face as she examined it. Eyes wide with shock, her pale skin flushed even whiter.

Stunned himself, Miguel tried to keep his voice free of panic. "Camille… Camille, can you talk to me?"

Whether she heard him or not, the older woman continued to stare at her arm stump. Blood splattered across her chest and down the sides of her neck in thick spurts. Her cries had now evolved into stuttering breaths.

"*Camille!*" he shouted. "Look at me."

Slowly, her head dropped to the side. Their eyes met, though Miguel wasn't sure if she even saw him.

"Camille, listen to me, okay? Can you hear me?"

EVERYBODY WANTS TO RULE THE WORLD

She continued to stare, her breaths becoming more labored and rapid.

"We're going to get out of this, okay? We're going to get out of this. You just have to trust me, yeah? Do you trust me?"

Camille's eyes began to close. Her arm dropped to her side. Blood raced across the carpeted floor. "I… I can't…"

Miguel's heart raced. He tried to lift his body, but the weight of the sheet metal duct kept him in place. He yanked his pinned arm, and a flurry of red-hot pain stopped him dead. Miguel ceased his struggles and returned his eyes to Camille.

She hadn't moved. Her eyes were not closed. Her mouth moved almost robotically, but he couldn't hear her words.

"Camille!" he cried. "Don't give up! Wake up, Camille! Wake up! Stay with me!"

Something a few floors above them crashed and shook what was left of the ceiling above. A hunk of concrete the size of a basketball dropped loose and fell directly onto Camille's head. She never made a noise as the solid mass crushed her skull, instantly pulping her face.

Miguel made all the noises for her. He looked away and screamed hard, willing the image of her impacted skull away. But it remained, playing over and over in his mind's eye. In a blind panic, Miguel once again attempted to use his only able arm to free himself. And the more he tried, the more his arm bled, and eventually, the pain became too much, and he blacked out.

✳

"Hey, get a load of the *retard*!"

The moment the word hit his ears, an icy shiver dripped uncomfortably down his spine. It wasn't even necessarily the word itself that got him. Boys his age were known to freely throw around hateful language for the sake of laughs and chauvinism. It was, unfortunately, a form of bonding and showmanship, and, despite its connotation, often a form of endearment amongst young boys who should probably know better. That didn't mean it was right, but most parents didn't bother to correct such language with much more than a stern look or a firm bark of their first and middle names.

No, it wasn't really the word itself that got him.

It was the added dose of venom that forced Miguel to turn around in his seat.

Like clockwork, the school bus trundled down the back wooded highway going far too fast, their elderly driver seemingly hitting nearly every bump and pothole she could manage. Mrs. Donaldson was long past retirement age and only used this job as her way of getting out of the house after her husband had passed away. She could barely see or hear, but even if she could, she never appeared to pay much attention to the rowdy teenagers she drove to and from Rice Middle School. At that age, many of Miguel's peers refused to follow any of the rules plastered to the wall by the front and back bus doors, using what little time away from class to roam the narrow walkway between the seats and openly gossip. Miguel wasn't sure if it was the raucous chatter or the deafening groans from the bus's shocks that hid

EVERYBODY WANTS TO RULE THE WORLD

Rocky Saul's repulsive slur. Either way, he appeared to be the only one who had heard it.

Well, he and Stevie O'Neill.

Sitting two rows back from Miguel, on the other side of the walkway in the last seat, was Rocky and another kid Miguel didn't recognize. Miguel was immediately confused as to why Rocky Saul was even on their bus to begin with, seeing as how he lived on the other side of town. He and his friend were obviously on the wrong bus, but if that was a purposeful decision or by dumb luck, Miguel couldn't be sure. Both reasons seemed passable. Rocky Saul was not the sharpest pencil in the desk, but what he lacked in common sense, he more than made up with in attitude and defiance. He was what Miguel's father referred to as an *alborotador*, or troublemaker, and urged him to leave those types to themselves. Miguel tended to agree, though he wasn't always so lucky. Being Puerto Rican, he was often the target of teasing and bullying, and he would just as often have to remind those *alborotadors* he wasn't exactly the type to take their shit.

Unlike Miguel, Stevie O'Neill couldn't defend himself.

He was one of the few kids in their school with Down syndrome, and he happened to live two streets over from Miguel. Everyone mostly left him alone, letting him come and go on his own with ease. He normally sat in the back of the bus near Miguel. Sometimes they would chat, but Stevie would mostly keep to himself, preferring to shuffle and count his stack of plastic-sleeved Pokémon cards.

Sitting in the last bench seat behind him, Rocky Saul and his friend leaned over the backrest, glaring. Impish grins split both their faces in two.

Rocky repeated, "I *said*, get a load of the *retard*!" He glanced around the bus, scanning to see if he had gotten a reaction from anyone. When no one responded, he stood up straighter in his seat and leaned down further into Stevie's airspace. "Ah, look at him, Greg. Playing with trading cards like he's all normal and shit. I'll bet the retard doesn't even know how to play them."

His friend, Greg, giggled and nodded.

If Stevie heard them, he gave no indication. He continued to shuffle his brightly colored deck, working the cards between his fingers.

"Hey, retard!" Rocky shouted, smacking the back of Stevie's head. "I'm talking to you. You *can* speak English, right?"

Stevie's eyes went wide with fright. His bottom lip curled inward.

Miguel had had enough. He quickly stood and exited his seat, taking three long steps until he was standing next to Stevie. "That's enough!"

Maybe they weren't expecting anyone to actually do or say anything, but Rocky and Greg nearly fell back in their seats in shock. When they realized they were taller than Miguel, they both leapt back up, their smiles instantly returning.

Rocky said, "Speaking of English, I'm shocked this little *beaner* knows any. *Hablas inglés, puta?*"

Not wanting to show his anger, Miguel stood silently as they snickered. This wasn't a new thing for him. He'd been made fun of and been picked on his whole life, simply because of his Spanish descent. Kids had a tendency to be cruel to those who didn't look like them and they had no problem loudly pointing it out. He always hoped the older he got, the less this would happen, but there would always be guys like Rocky Saul to defiantly remind him of their differences.

"I can speak English just fine," Miguel retorted in an even-keeled tone. "And unlike you, I don't need to resort to ugly name-calling to get my point across."

Greg finally spoke up. "And what point would that be, dickhead?"

"That you need to leave him alone."

Rocky's eyebrows rose. "Oh yeah?"

Miguel nodded. "And get off at the next stop and walk home."

There was a moment of silence before both erupted into forced laughter. Their cackles echoed throughout the crowded school bus. If they weren't paying attention before, most of their peers were now turned in their seats to watch.

"Goddamn, you're funny, man," Rocky said. He dismissively waved his hand, shooing Miguel like a bad dog. "Get back in your lane and sit down, funny man. What we're doing here? This doesn't concern you." He reached back and went to slap Stevie in the back of his head once more.

Before he could connect, Miguel swiftly smacked the other boy's hand, sending it away from Stevie. Stevie didn't so much as flinch. He remained seated, focusing solely on his playing cards.

Rocky growled, "*Mother fucker*... I said this doesn't concern you."

"If it has to do with Stevie O'Neill, then yeah, it does."

"What is he, your brother or some shit?" Greg snipped. "Don't look much like you."

Miguel kept his eyes directly on Rocky. "I said leave him alone and get off at the next stop. I won't tell you again."

"Oh?" Rocky asked. "You're not *asking* me? You're *telling* me?"

"Exactly."

Rocky slowly reached over the seat and snatched Stevie's cards from his grip. Other than a short grunt, Stevie didn't move. Bending the cards vertically in his grip, he shoved his hand in Miguel's face. A moment later, he let them go and a torrent of cardboard and plastic shot onto his eyes.

The entire bus went quiet. Even the bus itself seemed to stop moving.

The only thing that wasn't silent were the two young men in the back of the vehicle, cackling with laughter.

While the cards were still falling to the floor, Miguel seized the moment. He lashed out with a fist and struck Rocky directly in the nose. The bigger kid was still laughing as his nose cartilage flattened, unable to yelp until it was too late. He immediately collapsed to the seat, blood gushing from his reddened nostrils. Greg yelled something before trying to jump over the leather backrest toward Miguel. Miguel expected this and countered, using both hands to push the other kid backwards into his seat. Greg's head snapped back and struck the window behind him. The glass pane immediately splintered. Writhing on the bench, Greg screamed in pain, holding his head.

Unlike Greg, Rocky sat still in his spot. He stared up at Miguel, a mix of surprise and shock lighting his features. Bright blood continued to gush down his face, staining his jacket and shirt. "Bravo, funny man."

The bus shrieked to a halt. The driver shouted and grabbed for her radio.

Miguel knew he was in deep shit, but he didn't care. He despised bullying—loathed it—and wanted to put an end to it, which he did. Unless both other boys decided to jump him now and further their harassment, the event, as far as he was concerned, was settled.

He looked down at Stevie. "You okay, bud?"

Stevie, still staring ahead at the back of the seat in front of him, only nodded. Then together, they went to collecting his loose card deck off the floor.

Somewhere above him, Miguel heard Rocky mumble, "Bravo."

The roar of the fire seemed to penetrate his dreams. It filled his ears with a white noise so heavy and consistent it could have always been there. The room sweltered in the intense heat, boiling like an oven. While his right eye was still swollen shut, Miguel could barely open his left. The direct warmth stung him, immediately bringing forth tears, making him wince. That wince quickly became a scream when he tried to sit up. He had forgotten his arm had been forcefully immobilized by rebar. Blood continued to weep from his upper arm, pooling in a ruddy, coagulated blob on the rough carpet beneath him.

Despite the pain, Miguel knew he couldn't lay there forever. There was no telling what had happened or just how long he'd been trapped, but it was clear there was no one coming to rescue him. Even if someone was on their way, who knew if they could even make it up to nearly the top of the building to find him. He was on the sixteenth floor of the high-rise, smack dab in the center of the city. Between weekend traffic and perpetual road construction on the interstate, there was no telling where emergency workers could be at that point.

There was also the fire.

When he stirred awake, the flames had already moved from the floor above and were steadily devouring the walls of the workspace, swallowing everything they touched. From his vantage point, it wouldn't be long before the fire found the carpet and worked its way toward him.

Panic immediately seized him.

With a groan, Miguel used his free arm and, pushing upward with his knees, began to shove the air conditioning duct off his midsection. Another scream ripped through his raw throat. It was so much heavier than it looked, and with the corner touching the ground entertaining thick piles of ceiling work which weighed it down, it felt next to impossible to move. More tears rolled down his cheeks. When the duct refused to move, Miguel dropped his arms and knees and began to cry. Beneath the metal, his body quaked in anger and hurt, his chest hitching with sobs. He did not want to die like this. He wanted to die old, very old, surrounded by the faces of his friends and loved ones. There was still so much life to live. He wanted to get married and have kids and travel and see the world and do all that sentimental, corny shit they do in the movies. He wanted to experience it all. He wanted to live—not to die as a thirty-six-year-old on the job.

He lay there for a few more minutes, forcing himself to calm down and steady his erratic breathing. He closed his eye and took long, deep breaths, inhaling the intense heat. The flames around him crackled and popped, whispering to one another. Above him, metal framework groaned uncomfortably. A light breeze licked the room. Paper fluttered. And there was something else. Something further away. Somewhere outside. Not voices, but…

A short whimper suddenly hit his ears.

Immediately perking up, Miguel's good eye shot open. His heart raced. Was there someone in here actually still alive?

"H-hello?" he coughed. "Is there anyone else here?"

No one responded.

Shaking again, Miguel held his breath and listened. Background noises faded, and underneath, the short, pained breaths of someone nearby found him. Instead of responding, he laid there for several long moments, listening, studying, convincing himself that what he actually heard was just that—someone was indeed still living.

Adrenaline now surging, Miguel forgot his own pain. He thrust it out of his body as he let out a deep, bellowing groan and used his knees to push up. The air conditioning duct responded with its own sharp, indignant protest as it lifted off Miguel's midsection. One foot... Two feet... When he couldn't push any higher, he used his free arm and, grabbing the edge, pushed it upwards at arm's length. He let out one more grunt, then swung the duct sideways, clear of his body, then dropped it. Miguel sucked in a deep, uneasy breath, relishing the freedom to fully breathe once more. Not wanting to waste time, he rolled onto his side and delicately lifted the bundle of rebar off his arm. The broken skin beneath continued to freely bleed as he tossed the steel aside. Lightheadedness swept over him, and the intense pain came riding in with it. The wound wasn't as deep as he'd thought, but it was long and wide, covering at least six inches of reddened flesh. On his knees, Miguel searched for something to wrap his arm with. He found his long-sleeve shirt he normally left on the back of his chair and used a pair of scissors to cut one of the sleeves right off. He then gingerly wrapped his arm, right above the wound, and pulled it as tight as he could. The opening continued to bleed, but the flow dramatically reduced. Given the situation, that's all Miguel could ask for.

When the pain dulled and he felt like he could move, Miguel climbed unsteadily to his feet. To his surprise, the room was in much worse shape than he thought. The fire above continued to rage, while the floor around him was full of charred debris. What was once standing was now horizontal, broken and sprinkled around haphazardly like daycare toys. Desks and chairs had been destroyed, computers smashed and halved. The windows on the far wall were all but smashed, the view overlooking the city now covered in hundreds of spider-webbed cracks. Various desk ornaments, personal items, and framed pictures of loved ones were scattered about the floor like trash in a gutter.

Not that those loved ones would ever see their friends and family again.

Dozens of his co-workers' bodies were littered throughout the office floor. Many had been crushed in the explosion by the furniture around them, but the ones who sat directly under the blast had been hit by the fire. Their charred corpses continued to burn, their noxious fumes filling his nose. Splashes of dark blood were caked across the carpet.

Miguel choked back a sob. For the first time since the initial blast, he finally had the mental wherewithal to wonder just what the hell had happened. He tried to remember the events leading up to it. Nothing odd or suspicious immediately came to mind. He woke up, went to work, had a late breakfast, was finishing up his reports, then… *Boom.* Just another normal day before the ceiling above came crashing down. So…what happened? Maybe their building had been hit by a plane? *No*, he thought, looking around. *Otherwise, I'd see aircraft parts.* So what then? Mechanical failure? Electrical fire? Gas leak? It could have been any number of things, but the bodies that laid strewn about the floor didn't care. They were all dead regardless of the reason, and they weren't going home at the end of the work day to watch their favorite TV shows or to eat dinner or to fall asleep next to their wives or husbands. Parents wouldn't see their children grow older. Lonely pets would remain at the window. The horror of the situation came crashing down on Miguel's psyche, and the weight of survivor's guilt nearly toppled him. Unlike most of them, he had no one to go home to, no wife or girlfriend to cuddle next to on the couch, to enjoy takeout with, to make love with as the night wound down to bedtime. Just like he was in that very moment, he was all alone.

But he wasn't.

From the corner of his eye, he saw a flash of movement. It suddenly dawned on him he had forgotten what had gotten him up in the first place. He wasn't alone. Someone else was still alive.

He zig-zagged through the mess toward the far back corner of the room. There, he found a woman beneath her overturned desk, her legs pinned down by the heavy office furniture. Her dark brown skin was slick with sweat, as the wall ten feet away from her position was fully engulfed in flames. Miguel had never seen her before. She could have been new to the job, or maybe new to his area, but he couldn't put a name to her face. She looked young, maybe in her early twenties, though he couldn't be sure. Her eyes were closed tight, and her breaths came in harsh stutters. She was awake, but she made no move to free herself. Instead, her hands were held at her chest, her palms up, thumbs out, and index and pinkie up while the middle and ring fingers were down. Tears streamed down her cheeks.

Grunting, Miguel dropped to his knee beside her. "Ma'am? Ma'am, are you hurt? Can you get up?"

Finally acknowledging his presence, her eyes stayed closed but her breathy cries increased. "N-no."

"No what, ma'am? No you're not hurt, or no you can't get up?"

EVERYBODY WANTS TO RULE THE WORLD

"Leave… Leave me be."

Miguel was shocked. "Excuse me? I don't understand."

She shook her head. "Please, just leave me be."

"Ma'am, please let me help you up." The room began to swelter, the fire on the wall gnawing toward them with every passing second. Miguel placed a reassuring hand on her shoulder. "Let me just move the desk—"

"*No!*" she screamed, startling Miguel. Her bloodshot eyes opened and rolled toward him. Tears continued to spill down her cheeks, but her hands remained where they were, holding her rigid fingers in place. "Please. It hurts too much." Her stare then moved to the ceiling. "Just let me die in peace."

Miguel swallowed, the words unable to form. Despite the intense heat, a chill ran down his spine. She was obviously in a great deal of pain, but he refused to leave her here. He had to figure out how to get her up and moving. The longer they stayed, the greater the chances the room would fully engulf in flames. Miguel shot a glance at the wall. Deep, uneasy fissures snaked across the foundation, disappearing down through the floor and into the area below them. If the walls gave out, there was a great chance the roof over their heads—or what was left of it—would come crashing down. If that happened, the whole building would probably go.

Time was running short.

Heart hammering, Miguel returned his focus to the woman on the floor. "Okay, listen. We can't stay here. The longer we wait, the worse off we'll be, so we really need to get you up and on your feet. Sound good?"

She didn't answer.

"What's your name? How about we start off with that?"

A few seconds passed before she answered, "Sue."

"Sue." He nodded, touching her shoulder. "Good. That's a good start, Sue. I'm Miguel. It's nice to meet you, Sue." When she didn't respond, he asked, "Are you in pain, Sue? What hurts?"

"My...my legs."

"Okay, your legs. That's very understandable. Look, I want to help you, Sue, but I'm going to need *your* help, okay? I'm going to need you to assist me in lifting this desk off you. I can't do it all on my own." He showed her the homemade tourniquet on his arm. "I'm hurt too. I'll need you to help push."

Sue shook her head, biting her lip. "I can't."

"You can't? What do you mean you can't?"

"I want to keep my hands...just like this."

Miguel shook his head, confused. "I don't understand, Sue. Why are your hands like that?"

Her puffy eyes met his. "My daughter. She's deaf. When they find me, I want her to know I was thinking of her before I died. They say, 'I love you.'"

It was now Miguel's turn to cry. He had never heard anything so devastating in his life. He had no idea who this woman was, yet those few words told a life's worth of story...a story he refused to see end like this. This woman, his co-worker, Sue, would not die like this. He had no idea what had caused this hell to be handed down to them, but all he knew was that they were going to make it out of this room, of this building, and Sue would see her child again, if it was the last thing he ever did.

26

EVERYBODY WANTS TO RULE THE WORLD

Miguel wiped his eye and gently laid his hands over hers. "Sue, listen to me. I'm not going to let you die today. You hear me? I'm not going to let you die. I'm going to help you up, and we're going to get the hell out of here and get you back to your daughter. Does that sound good?"

Sue's chest hitched with sobs. Miguel expected her to continue her protests and refuse his aid, but when her bout of crying ended, she simply nodded.

"Good," he said, squeezing her fingers. He eyed the desk on her legs. "Okay, Sue, I'm going to need you to talk to me. Just talk to me while I work on getting this off you. Focus on my voice. Don't think about anything else. Does that work for you?"

"Yeah," she croaked.

"Excellent." Miguel stood and flexed his fingers. While his left arm was good to go, his wounded arm remained numb and fairly useless. He would have to do this one-handed. Crouching, he slipped his hand underneath the overturned top. "What's your daughter's name?"

"It's… It's Jean."

"That's a beautiful name."

"Thank you."

"Are you married?" He began to lift the desk, surprised by the weight. "Boyfriend, girlfriend?"

Sue cried out in pain but managed to answer through gritted teeth. "*Boyfriend*."

Miguel grunted as he strained to lift it higher. He tried to grasp with his right hand, but his numb fingers refused to hold. "Does he have a name?"

"Gene."

Miguel bit back a laugh. "Jean and Gene?"

"Didn't plan it that way," she groaned.

Giving it his all, Miguel lifted the hefty piece of furniture clear of her legs. He shoved the desk as hard as he could, sending it toppling away. Prone on the floor, Sue screamed in agony. Miguel couldn't be quite sure, but one or both of her legs may have been broken. They wouldn't know until he got her on her feet.

"Sue, focus and talk to me, okay? How long have you been working here?"

"*It hurts so goddamn bad!*"

Miguel knelt back down next to her. "Sue, come on! Look at me. Please."

Breathing heavily, Sue wiped her eyes and stared up at him.

"Good. How long have you been working here?"

"Th-three days."

"Three days? I see. *That's* why I haven't really seen you before." Grabbing her by the forearm, Miguel eased Sue up to a sitting position.

"I started on Wednesday."

"How are you liking it so far?"

She pulled a face. "It's not great."

"Yeah, it's not always like this. Sometimes, Wilburn brings in pizzas for us on Fridays."

When Sue barked out a sarcastic laugh, Miguel took the distraction and swiftly pulled her to her feet. Sue immediately bellowed in pain, and Miguel quickly snaked his left arm around her shoulders and pulled her up. Miguel felt her go slack in his hold, her knees giving out, but he held her firm and upright.

EVERYBODY WANTS TO RULE THE WORLD

"*My right knee!*" she squealed, teeth bared. "I-I think it's b-broken!"

"Stay with me, Sue. How old is she?"

Sue shot him a bewildered look. "*What?*"

"Your daughter? Jean? How old is she?"

"She's… Oh, fuck, it hurts…"

"Stay calm, Sue. It's going to be okay."

A large chunk of flaming ceiling tile fell to their left, sending sparks flying like fireworks. The carpet immediately caught fire and rapidly began to spread.

Mind racing, Miguel was having a hard time following his own advice to remain composed. While he was helping his office mate, the room had promptly become an inferno. The ceiling, the walls, the overturned furniture…all now consumed in a very realistic hell. The bodies of their co-workers, those saved from this view, were not spared by the flames. Reds and yellows bubbled their flesh, blackening everything around them. It would only be a matter of minutes before the fires completely overtook the room, making any sort of escape impossible. They had to move.

As if hearing his thoughts, the entire building shook. The cracks on the walls opened wider. Above them, the remains of the ceiling commenced to bow inward.

The floors above them were about to come down.

Miguel swallowed hard. "We have to leave." He looked down into Sue's face. "*Now!*"

Sue did not protest.

Together, they hobbled toward the middle of the room, where the fire had yet to touch. From what

Miguel could see, there were only three options. The elevator on the far side of the office, the main staircase located beyond the kitchen area, and the emergency stairs next to the back closet, for which he didn't have a key. The fires had already taken the space surrounding the elevator, so that wasn't an option. The main staircase was also a no-go, as the entire kitchen was now a pyre of burning equipment. That left them with the emergency stairs.

Key or not, it was their only shot out.

Making sure Sue was held tight, he swiftly guided her toward the door.

The building bellowed above them. A moment later, the ceiling lurched toward them—

They both screamed. Miguel forced them both into a crouch, throwing his body over hers, readying himself for the impact—

—but it never came.

Miguel glanced up. The ceiling had not completely come down, but it was nearly three feet lower than it had previously been. Three quarters of the room was now gone, consumed in flames, the heat now unbearable. Miguel returned his eye to the staircase door.

His heart sank.

The door had been nearly squashed. Though it was still mostly shut, the upper half had been smashed down, squashing the upper frame and bowing the door out toward them. The top hinge had snapped off, but the lower remained in place.

Miguel quickly pulled Sue to her feet and, despite her pained cries, led them forward.

EVERYBODY WANTS TO RULE THE WORLD

The ceiling once again groaned. The building tremored beneath them.

When they reached the door, Miguel twisted the knob and pulled.

Still locked.

"*No, no, no!*" he cried. "Open, goddamn it! *Open!*"

Sue screamed, "*It's coming down!*"

The ceiling was now gradually dropping, the office walls finally giving in to the pressure. Charred drywall burst onto the floor. Fires raced toward them. Concrete and metal rained down. The cacophony was deafening.

In a few moments, they would both be dead.

"*Perdóname…*"

Reacting to the weight, the emergency staircase door squealed as it snapped free from the final hinge. The lock snapped, and the door popped open, offering little more than a foot of room to squeeze past.

Wasting no time, Miguel thrust Sue toward the opening and pushed her through. As the ceiling came crashing down the rest of the way, erasing their workspace from existence, Miguel hastily slid through the door and into the darkness beyond.

After a week of nearly non-stop flurries and random bouts of icy sleet, old man winter had finally decided to hang up his boxing gloves. The entire Tri-state area had taken quite the beating. Businesses had been closed for days on end, restaurants begrudgingly suspended service, and even the local postal workers—despite their "through rain, sleet, or snow" motto—kept themselves safely at home. The shuttering of welcome doors also extended to schools of all levels, which Miguel was incredibly thankful for. Instead of stressing about his trigonometry grades or worrying if Morgan Kozeniewski was going to write him dirty notes all through Economics class, he happily loafed around the house instead. He ate everything in sight, knocked out a couple of books off his TBR pile, and stayed up late for days on end playing *Super Mario Bros.* on his older sister's Super Nintendo. For a seventeen-year-old high schooler, it was pure Heaven on Earth.

As soon as the snow died off, so did the good times.

What took ten days to cover the earth took only a day and a half of county plow work to clear the roads, which unfortunately meant school would be back in session straightaway. Miguel woke up early on Tuesday morning to check the TV, and just as he feared, the scrolling banner on the bottom of the morning news gleefully informed the waking world to finally get back to normal life. After begrudgingly packing his lunch, Miguel bundled up and waited outside for the bus.

Only the bus wasn't waiting for him.

"Get in, chucklehead!" Rocky called from his driver's side window.

Miguel immediately pulled a face. He quickly checked the house behind him, then grinned and did as he was told.

After years of trying to figure out how he and Rocky became close friends, Miguel ultimately decided it wasn't worth the effort. Somehow, after their tussle on the school bus five years prior, Rocky Saul had, for whatever reason, given up his ways. The once-problem child with a history of bullying and intolerance and suspensions became just that: history. Miguel had no idea what changed his tune. Maybe it was the fact that someone had finally, after years of pushing others around, gotten a taste of his own bitter medicine. Miguel supposed all it took was a fist to the beak and the tiger was instantly turned into a kitten. A now six-foot-two high school kitten with massive biceps…but a kitten nonetheless.

Soon after their altercation on the bus, Rocky had begun to randomly approach Miguel in the hallways at school. At first, he thought the bigger kid was seeking out revenge, ready to show Miguel exactly why he earned his reputation, but his advances were oddly affable. Without mentioning what had happened, Rocky would pop up at Miguel's locker or at his lunch table to simply chat about music or movies or whatever sport he was into at that time of year. Miguel was obviously guarded, unsure of what Rocky's intentions actually were. But after months of wearing him down, Miguel relented and began to warm up to this kid. It didn't take much time to grasp how lonely Rocky actually was. His friends were few and far between, and the entire teaching staff seemed to have given up on him all together. Maybe he just needed a friend. Someone to help him on to the straightened path and to be less of a shitheel. Miguel fancied himself a bit of a loner as well, so it was easy to sympathize with someone like Rocky Saul, despite his questionable character. Though there was never a formal apology to or for his actions toward

Stevie O'Neill, Miguel decided it was, for now, water under the bridge.

The car was nice and toasty when Miguel hopped inside. "I see you finally got the heater fixed."

"Sure looks that way." Rocky pulled away from the curb and headed out of Miguel's neighborhood, going a bit too fast.

Miguel quickly buckled in. "You good, bro?"

Despite the slush still lingering on the roads, Rocky floored the gas and raced around street corners like he was going for a medal. Miguel, teeth gritted, placed one hand on the dash and another around the door handle.

When Rocky didn't answer, Miguel repeated, "Yo, Rock, you okay, man?"

Without looking his way, the teenaged driver answered, "Miggy, I couldn't be any fucking better if I tried."

Miguel knew sarcasm when he heard it. "You don't have to bullshit me, bro. What's up?"

"I said I'm *fine*!"

The air in the vehicle instantly went from warm to unpleasantly chilly. For what it was worth, Rocky had not so much as raised his voice in anger toward Miguel in some time. As far as he knew, his friend had been on his best behavior for years, avoiding all fights both verbal and physical. Miguel didn't want to take the credit for Rocky's change in behavior, but he sure liked to think he helped in some small way.

After a few minutes of awkward silence, Rocky finally spoke up. "My, uh, my parents... They're getting a divorce."

EVERYBODY WANTS TO RULE THE WORLD

"Well shit, man. I'm really sorry to hear that."

"Yeah. Me too."

Miguel wasn't sure what to say. "You…okay?"

His friend side-eyed him and pursed his lips. "I'll live."

"Do you want to talk about it?"

"Why do you think I picked you up, dummy?" Shaking his head, Rocky spat, "That *fucking* bitch…"

Scenarios running through his head, Miguel asked, "So…what happened?"

Rocky croaked out a dry laugh. "I'll tell you what happened, good buddy. I'll tell you exactly what happened. My dad caught my fucking whore mother cheating on him. That's what the fuck happened."

Miguel grimaced at Rocky's choice of words. "Geeze, bro. I'm sorry to hear that."

"And *that's* not even the worst part."

"Oh?"

Rocky angrily punched the steering wheel. "She's been fucking some Black guy!"

Miguel turned to his friend with a perplexed look. "Excuse me?"

"I know, *right?* I couldn't believe it myself when Dad told me. Totally out of left field, man."

"No, I meant 'Excuse me' as in 'Why does that matter?'"

Now it was Rocky's turn to look confused. "I don't follow."

"What I'm saying is why does it matter if he's Black or not? What does the guy's skin color have anything to do with it?"

Bewilderment enveloped Rocky's face. "Because... Because it fucking does!"

The car began to speed up, racing down the highway.

Miguel turned his body to face his friend. "No, Rock, it *doesn't*. Look, I get it. You're upset and you're looking for something to aim your anger at. Seriously, I get it. But him being Black has nothing to do with anything."

"Like hell it doesn't!"

"Your anger is misplaced, man. Be furious, be upset. That's okay. That's natural. I'm sure I would be feeling the same shit if I was in your shoes, but there's no need to bring his race into this, and you know it."

Rocky could only glance back and forth from the road to his passenger, his upper lip curled slightly in a sneer.

"Listen, man," Miguel continued. "I've been fucked with my whole life for being Puerto Rican. Just because of my dark skin, people immediately have some sort of preconceived notions of who I am and what I represent in this world. Do you have any idea how many times I've been called a *beaner* and a *wetback* and a *spic* just because of the way I look? It's absolutely dehumanizing. It makes me feel like shit, Rock. They don't know me. They don't know who I am or what I've gone through or where I've been. They just see my complexion and immediately pass a blind judgement." Miguel shook his head. "Not to mention, those are Mexican slurs. If you're going to insult me, at the very least use the right terms."

EVERYBODY WANTS TO RULE THE WORLD

After a few moments of silence, a grin snaked across Rocky's lips. "Wait, so you're not Mexican?"

"Fuck you, man." Miguel turned forward in his seat with a smile. "Look, all I'm saying is, it's fucked up what's happening with your parents, but leave that dude out of it. Be angry at your mom, not him."

Something odd dawned on Miguel. Throughout their conversation, he had not been paying the slightest bit of attention to where they were headed. He realized they should have been at school by now, parked and already in the building. Instead, they were now much further down the highway, nearing the opposite end of town.

Miguel asked, "Yo, where are we going?"

Rocky simply shrugged.

"Asshole, we're supposed to be at school! Where are you taking me?"

"Somewhere special."

"Come on, man," Miguel yelled with a sigh. "We can't just skip today. My dad will tear my ass up if he finds out I played hooky."

"Jesus Christ!" Rocky shouted. "Would you live a little, you goddamn baby? We're seniors, Miggy. We graduate in, like, three months! Who gives a flying fuck if we ditch school for a day? What—are they going to give us detention? Withhold our diplomas? Hold us back another year? Give me a break, man. Just enjoy the day with me, okay? Take the stick out of your Mexican ass and have a little adventure with me."

Rolling his eyes, Miguel crossed his arms and sank back in his seat. "Fine. Whatever. So, where are we going? It better be worth it if we're both going to get grounded."

Rocky simply answered, "You'll see."

Ten minutes later, they were slowly pulling into a small cul-de-sac near the opposite edge of town. The neighborhood was still mostly covered in snow, the city plows seemingly having not made it to that end quite yet. The houses were small, mostly single story, and the driveways were all but barren. Save for one. A green Dodge truck sat idling beneath the open carport.

Rocky carefully pulled his car up in front of the house next to it and parked. "Here we are."

Miguel eyed the quiet neighborhood suspiciously. "And...where is *here*?"

Leaving the car running, Rocky leapt out of the car without a word.

"Rock?" Miguel quickly joined him outside. "Dude, what are we doing?"

His friend knelt down in the street and began to form tightly packed snowballs in his hands. "I'll tell you what we're doing, Miggy. You see that piece of shit truck right there?"

Miguel nodded, his stomach tightening by the second.

"And do you see that piece of shit house that that piece of shit truck is sitting near?"

"Get to the point, Rock."

After balling up about ten snowballs, Rocky reached into his jacket pocket and extracted a handful of large stones. One by one, he pushed them inside the snowballs, then gave them a courtesy roll in his hands to smooth over the surface. After he finished, he laid them all on the hood of his car, side by side.

EVERYBODY WANTS TO RULE THE WORLD

He turned toward Miguel with a wry smile. "Well, my friend, the piece of shit who owns both of those pieces of shit just so happens to be the very same piece of shit that's been fucking my mother."

It didn't take Miguel long to put two and two together. "*No, no, no!* Absolutely not!"

Rocky rolled his eyes and knelt back down to make more weaponized snowballs.

Panicked, Miguel leaned forward to sweep away the ones Rocky had already created, but his friend quickly stood and used his overwhelming size to tower over him.

"*Leave them be!*" His words echoed in the morning air, somehow forming a cloud of antagonistic vitriol between them.

Miguel had never been afraid of Rocky Saul. Not when they first met on the bus, and not even now, when his swollen teenage arms bulged beneath his track jacket. But something, some inane sense of vulnerability, forced him to hold back.

"I get to have this, Miggy." Rocky appeared to be fighting back tears. "I get to have this."

"What are you going to do? Damage his property? Break some windows? Where's that going to leave you other than jail, man?"

"*I don't fucking care!* That fucking guy broke my family apart! My parents are getting separated because of him!" He saw Miguel begin to object, so he spoke over him. "And I don't want to hear your self-righteous horseshit about taking the high road or blame my mom and not him or let my parents figure their mess out on their own or whatever. I don't want to hear it! I've been a good little boy for a long fucking time, Miggy—a long fucking time. I've been on my best behavior, I have, but I'm hurting, man. I'm fucking hurting." The tears finally came loose and dripped down his reddened cheeks. "You're absolutely right. About all of that shit. You are. And that's what I love about you, man. You've kept me an honest man for a long time now. But right now, Miggy? Right now I have to do this. I don't care about the consequences or what happens after."

Miguel continued to stare at his friend, unblinking.

"Just let me do this one goddamn thing. Let me get it out of my system, and I swear it will never happen again, okay? I need this for my sanity, man."

After a few moments of hopeless refection, Miguel put up his hands in surrender and turned away.

The front door to the house opened, and a large man stepped outside. He stopped in place when he eyed the two of them.

"Can I help you?"

Rocky exploded.

In a flash, he swept up a handful of snowballs and took several long strides toward the man. Then, one by one, he began to lob them as hard as he could.

"*You mother fucking piece of shit! You cock sucking scumbag!*"

The rock-filled snowballs fell upon the man, striking him hard in the midsection. As he tried to dodge the onslaught, he roared back at Rocky, but his words barely made it over Rocky's own cries.

"*You broke my family apart, you cheating son of a bitch! You destroyed my fucking family!*"

EVERYBODY WANTS TO RULE THE WORLD

Snowball after snowball struck the man, the rocks inside giving them weight and substance. To Miguel, the whole ordeal looked completely ridiculous, like an angry child throwing a tantrum the only way he knew how, but it was so much more than that. Despite the absurdity, Rocky was actually hurting him. He trudged closer to the man, who was now curled up on his front lawn, and hurled his remaining snowballs directly into his face. The man screamed and writhed, his face gushing bright blood across the dirty white snow.

Fear gripping him, Miguel rushed for Rocky and attempted to pull him away. "Let's go, man! You've done enough! Let's go!"

Now empty handed, Rocky leaned forward and bellowed directly into the man's wounded face. "*Get near my mother again and I'll fucking kill your black ass! Do you understand me? I said do you understand me, you fucking bitch?*"

As Rocky continued to rave, Miguel successfully drug him backwards toward his car. He pushed Rocky into the driver's seat and then hopped into the opposite side, and a moment later, they were back on the road.

Miguel found he could not stop shaking. His heart hammered, and his stomach spun like a pinwheel. He had never seen such hateful violence up close, so explicit and raw. No matter how many times he blinked, he couldn't rid the image of that man's bleeding face and his pleading eyes.

From the driver's seat, Rocky began to laugh. It started as a throaty chuckle, then quickly morphed into hysterical cackling.

Miguel stared at his friend in shock.

Rocky turned to Miguel with a bright red face.

"Well, that was fucking intense, wasn't it?" Laugher swept over him once more.

Too stunned to respond, Miguel simply hugged himself in the cold passenger seat, where not even the heater could warm him.

❋

Normally, their footsteps would have echoed throughout the barren stairwell, each footfall reverberating like gunshots, but the slowly collapsing infrastructure nearly swallowed their movements whole. The raging fires, only a few floors above them, were now a continuous dull roar. As Miguel helped carry Sue down step by careful step, the sound was a wretched reminder that their time—however long that may be—was running short.

The terrified woman Miguel clung tightly to groaned repeatedly as they proceeded together down the narrow staircase. She kept her right knee crooked up, not daring to let her foot touch the ground. Miguel was still in a great deal of pain himself. Despite the sloppy tourniquet, which he perhaps tied too tightly, his arm throbbed painfully, as if it had its own separate heart. He loosened the fabric around his arm and tried to flex his fingers, but they had gone completely numb. His right eye remained swollen shut, but his left wasn't much help. It remained wet and leaky, irritated by the mounting smoke and fire. He prayed to God he wouldn't lose his sight.

Sue began to cry again. Her chest hitched with sobs, her body trembling next to his.

EVERYBODY WANTS TO RULE THE WORLD

"Tell me about Jean," Miguel said, breaking their silence.

Sue wiped her nose. "My boyfriend?"

Miguel smirked. "Your daughter."

"Right." Despite her pain, Sue immediately lit up. "She's the sweetest little girl in the whole world. The whole wide world. She's so smart and so full of personality. She's got more character than most adults I know."

"She sounds awesome, Sue."

Sue glanced up at him with a smile. "She is indeed."

"You never did tell me how old she was."

"Oh. Yeah. She's six."

Miguel nodded. "That's a great age. They're old enough to really play with and teach and talk to… Shit, I'm sorry."

She waved him off. "It's okay. I know what you mean. It is a great age. We're past the terrible twos, and now she's so mature and independent, even with her disability. She's such a trooper, you know?"

"Very happy to hear that. I hope I get to meet her one day."

Miguel eased them both onto the next landing and paused to catch his breath. He closed his eye and swallowed, desperately wishing he had some water to cleanse his dry throat.

"Can we just stop here for a bit?" Sue eventually asked. "I'm not sure how much more I can keep going."

"I would love nothing more than that, but we can't. The way that ceiling came down on us? I don't want to take the chance on us sitting still and the whole building coming down on our heads."

"God, it hurts so much."

"I know, Sue. Believe me I know." Miguel opened his eye and turned to look at her. "We're going to get out of here."

She eyed him. "Are we?"

"Do you trust me?"

"You saved my life. So yes."

"If it's the last thing I do, I'm going to get you back to your daughter. Okay?"

Sue bit her lip, more tears running down her face. She nodded. "Thank you, Miguel. You're a good man. God bless you."

"Don't thank me yet."

"Hey," she said, looking around. "Why haven't we seen any other people? Workers from the offices?"

"Most of the other businesses are closed on Saturdays. Us and only a few other offices run on the weekends. Maybe five or six altogether, I think. Cleaning staff isn't even here today." He pointed up. "All those other doors we passed going down? I didn't bother checking them because they're all locked over the weekend."

"I just assumed there was no reason to since we're moving down."

"Yeah, that too."

Miguel noticed the smoke was getting thicker. "Hold on." He crept over to the railing and looked down.

His heart sank.

Thick grey smoke was beginning to billow out from the next landing, presumably from the floor just below them. He couldn't see or hear the fire quite yet, but he knew it was close.

EVERYBODY WANTS TO RULE THE WORLD

This isn't a coincidence, he thought miserably. *Something more is happening here…*

"What is it?" Sue asked. "What's happening? What do you see?"

Miguel hesitated before answering, "More fire, by the looks of it."

"No, no, no!" Breaking from his hold, she hobbled backwards until she awkwardly collided with the wall. "I can't do this again! I just can't!"

"Sue, we don't have a choice."

"Yes, we do! We can go through one of the other floors—"

Miguel turned her way. "And I already told you they're all locked. It's the weekend. Not a single one of those doors will open for us. That's just the way it is."

Panicking, Sue rapidly shook her head, her chest hitching with unmanageable sobs. "I can't do this… I can't do this…"

Grabbing her shoulders, he held her in place. "Sue, there's nothing we can do. We can't go back up. That's no longer an option, okay? All those doors are *locked*. They're no good to us. We don't have any other options but to go down."

"*There's got to be another way!*" she shrieked.

Miguel shook his head, keeping his voice free of impatience or alarm. "There isn't."

After a few more moments of heavy breathing, Sue eventually nodded. "Okay. Okay."

"You still trust me, right?"

Her teary eyes met his. "Yes."

"Good. Nothing's changed. I'm still going to get you back to your daughter. I promise."

Sue sucked in her lips. "Don't make promises like that. Ones you can't guarantee."

Miguel started to speak, but then thought better of it. He eased her arm over his shoulder and began to guide her toward the next set of descending stairs.

"One step at a time."

They had made it down two more flights before the smoke became too much. Coughing, they both pulled their shirts up over their noses and continued their descent. Miguel's only open eye stung so badly he could barely see, instead relying on Sue to navigate.

Soon, they could go no further.

They both halted on the final platform as they discovered that it was indeed the last platform they could traverse. Miguel's intuition had been correct. There was absolutely something much bigger happening here. It was obvious that another explosion had happened on the floor they were now at. The door had been blown off the hinges. Brick and steel surrounding the opening had been blown to pieces and scattered about their feet. The explosion must have been close because the staircase itself took a good bit of damage. Along with much of the platform, the two sets of stairs directly below them were gone, now a detached jumble of crooked steel laying on the platform a few floors below.

There was absolutely no way down.

"What do we do?" Sue asked.

He pointed to the opening. "Only one option. Through."

Though there were no flames around the opening, smoke continued to billow through the wall, filling the stairwell with gray, noxious fumes. Miguel, keeping them both low, stepped around the loose debris and carefully guided them both inside.

The floor was so much worse than he could have imagined.

Bodies were everywhere. While some remained fully intact, many had not been so fortunate. Detached appendages of all colors and sizes were scattered about the scorched floor and across the overturned cubicles and desks. A woman's severed head peeked out from underneath a chair, part of her shoulder and chest still attached to the ragged neck stump. A severed leg stood up against the wall, as if the owner had left it and hopped away. Sue cried out at the sight and closed her eyes. Miguel couldn't help but stare. So much unneeded death, so much destruction and chaos… For what?

The fires were mostly burnt down, but the walls had been blackened from the smoke, which continued to crackle and swell. On the far end of the room, the floor-to-ceiling plate glass windows were all gone, leaving several large openings into the outside world. A cool breeze whipped through the newly excavated office space, swirling the smoke and pushing it out into the sky. For a short while, Miguel relished the fresh air across his brow, not realizing until then how much he had been sweating. But there was something else… Something that came in with the wind and seized his troubled ears.

Sue whispered, "Do you hear that?"

"Yeah."

"Is…that what I think it is?"

Miguel licked his dry lips and swallowed. "Yep."

Somewhere down below, gunshots rang out in the afternoon air. They echoed in the distance, their abrupt, confident barks sending icy chills right down Miguel's spine.

Something much, much bigger is happening here...

A cough from somewhere nearby made them both jump.

Not wanting to waste a second of time, Miguel hurried Sue past the various dead bodies to the other side of the room. "Hello? Who's there? Where are you at?"

Another harsh cough turned into a bout of gagging as they frantically searched for the source.

"If you can talk," Miguel shouted, "please speak up so we can find you!"

When they reached the other end of the space, they stopped in front of the side office and found an arm waving lazily at them from behind a deluge of cabinets and broken chairs. The large office window had been blown inward, presumably by the explosion, leaving behind a yawning maw of jagged glass. Since the door was broken in half and unable to fully open, Miguel leaned Sue against the outside wall and then gingerly stepped inside through the window opening.

The room was a ruin and nearly impossible to traverse. His numb arm now throbbing with pain, Miguel quickly cleared a path to the side of the overturned work desk. The hand beneath the rubble had stopped moving, but the fingers laying on top of the filing cabinet flinched when Miguel drew near.

"Almost there," Miguel said, working on clearing the debris off the person. "Just hang tight."

He lifted the cabinet and stood it back upright. Underneath, he found an older white man leaning against the wall. His bald white head was covered in blood, shards of sparkling glass sticking out of his skull like thin, gleaming strands of hair. The man's eyes were wide with shock, his breath coming in short, shallow hitches.

Miguel sighed in relief. "Sir? Sir, are you okay? Can you move?"

The man was still staring ahead, breathing rapidly.

"Sir?" Miguel repeated, reaching out for the man's shoulder.

When Miguel's hand squeezed, the man flinched and turned his eyes toward him. "H-hello."

"Hi. Sir, are you okay? We've come to help you out of here."

Confusion washed over the man's features. "Help? W-w-what do you m-mean?"

"Sir, there's been an accident."

"An accident?" The man squinted at Miguel, studying him. "D-do y-you work here?"

He's obviously in shock, Miguel thought. "Well, yes. But not on this floor. I'm up on the sixteenth. Seidlinger and Headlee Industries."

"Seid... Ah yes. Y-you're one of W-Wilburn's."

"Yes, sir."

"Good man."

"Indeed. Sir, what's your name?"

"Rowland."

"It's very nice to meet you, Rowland. My name's Miguel Toro." Miguel knelt next to him. "Listen, I need to help you up so we can all get out of the building."

"Get…"

"Yes, get out. Are you in pain?"

Rowland didn't answer for a bit. His eyes seemed to cross as they stared off into the distance. "N-no... Just c-c-cold..."

Miguel nodded. "I understand. Look, I need to lift this desk off your body, okay? Are you able to push up?"

"No. I d-don't t-think s-so."

"That's okay. I believe I can lift it myself." Thankfully, after loosening the tourniquet, his numb arm was slowly beginning to regain some feeling. Flexing his fingers, he knelt down and maneuvered them underneath the lip of the wooden desk. "Ready?"

"Sure."

Grunting, Miguel began to lift. A moment later, he let out a cry and carefully eased the desk back down. His entire body flushed cold.

"Miguel?" Sue called from outside the room. "Everything okay?"

He only got a short look at the scene beneath the desk, but it was enough time to know he would never forget it.

When the bomb went off, not even being in his own private office could save Rowland from the concentrated destruction. While the others outside were instantly killed, the plate glass window that looked out into the main office had shattered from the explosion. The door had been blown to pieces, and large sections of glass had propelled inward...right into Rowland. Smaller shards had impaled him in various places, but his midsection had taken the absolute worst of it. In that split second, Miguel witnessed what appeared to be

EVERYBODY WANTS TO RULE THE WORLD

Rowland's glistening innards laying on the floor beneath him. Dark blood stained the carpet, gushing out of him rapidly. What bothered Miguel the most was seeing the man's lower half…which was sitting a few inches away from his upper half.

The glass had completely halved him.

Tears immediately burst from Miguel's eye. He backed away a foot and covered his mouth with his fist.

"Miguel?" Sue yelled. "What's going on?"

Now it was Miguel who was having trouble breathing. His heart hammered, his head swimming, stomach ready to void itself.

Below him, Rowland stared in confusion.

He doesn't know…

"Miguel!"

Calming himself, Miguel finally spoke up. "It… it's okay. We're okay. Just stay where you're at."

Rowland licked his cracked lips. "S-so c-cold."

Miguel wiped his eye and stepped back over to him. He had no idea what to say. "Listen…"

"Do you h-have a-an appointment?"

"No, Rowland. I don't. I'm sorry."

Rowland nodded, his eyes going crossed once more. "Okay."

"Rowland? Do… Do you have a wife or a partner I can get in touch with?"

"Wife?" he croaked. "N-no. My D-Dana passed a-away a few y-years ago."

"I'm so sorry to hear that."

Rowland looked down and pointed to the floor behind Miguel. "My p-phone."

51

Miguel followed his finger and found the man's cell phone on the carpet. He snatched it up and stared at it.

"It's m-my grandson's b-birthday," Rowland continued. "S-S-Sammy. He's seven today."

"That's a great age."

Rowland smiled. "H-he's an awesome k-kid. He's p-probably awake n-now. I want t-to call him on his…"

Tears once again burst from Miguel's eye. "That's a great idea, Rowland." He swiped the screen and opened the main page. "What's his number?"

Rowland didn't answer.

Beyond the phone, the old man had stopped breathing. His glazed-over stare looked blankly at Miguel, his mouth still open in mid-sentence. The silence between them was deafening.

After several long seconds, Miguel turned the phone's screen off and then stood and left the room.

"What?" Sue asked, glancing behind him. "What happened? Where is he?"

Miguel declined to answer.

"Rocky is…a complicated man."

All at once, the room erupted into sardonic laughter. It wasn't *that* funny of a joke, but Miguel supposed that at an event like this, one where the good times and alcohol were congruently manufactured, everything he said during his time with the microphone was expected to be humorous. That was fine by him. Seeing as how this would probably be his only opportunity, he took his job as best man very seriously.

The whole week had gone off without a hitch. Miguel worked closely with the Maid of Honor, Bridgett, and together, they were able to cooperate in getting all the finer wedding details ironed out with very little issues. While Rocky's bride-to-be, Gemma, had gone off to Vegas with her excitable bridesmaids, Rocky and his small group of groomsmen decided to take a short car trip to Louisville for his bachelor's party. And what a small group it was. Outside of his best man, Miguel, there were only two other guys in the party, one being a friend from college, and the other a guy he worked with at the manufacturing plant. He rounded out the groomsmen with his father and his uncle, but neither went over the border to Kentucky with them.

Miguel wasn't all that surprised Rocky had trouble picking a group of guys to take part in his wedding day. Outside of Miguel, he was fairly positive Rocky didn't actually have many—if any—real, close friends. Whoever he hung out with in high school didn't stick around after they took off for college. Most left town the moment summer was over, leaving him and Miguel behind to attend the local four year program. Miguel wasn't all that bothered by it. He was never close with anyone Rocky ran around with, but those few individuals deemed worthy enough weren't exactly the type he felt comfortable around anyways. Lower middle class white kids with loud opinions and louder mouths to shout them. They never really gave Miguel any grief, but the few times they were all together in a group, Miguel could tell he was the odd man out. That was fine with him. Outside of Rocky, the older Miguel got, the more he found himself a loner. He was okay with Rocky being one of his only actual companions.

Which was why he took so much pride in being Rocky's best man.

"I can tell by your laughter, you all know what I'm talking about."

Miguel glanced down at the happy couple next to him. Hand in hand, Rocky and Gemma Saul sat together on the raised stage with the rest of the wedding party. Gemma's strawberry blonde hair was twisted into a large, winding mess of curls that bushed over her shoulders, her face layered in meticulous makeup she would not have normally worn. She grinned up at Miguel as he spoke, yet her eyes seemed to hold some hesitation, as if she were fearful of what he was about to say. Rocky, on the other hand, didn't appear to care at all. Unlike his wife's painstaking efforts to make herself look her best, Rocky spent the day looking as though he'd just rolled out of bed. His hair, which had started to heavily recede in his early twenties, was uncombed and remained wherever the wind placed it. His flushed cheeks were peppered with several days of stubble. Even his rental suit was sloppy, untucked and wrinkled. Miguel could smell the alcohol on Rocky when he showed up at the church, and Rocky continued to drink throughout the morning into the reception. He was barely paying attention to Miguel's speech, instead whispering something to his co-worker two seats down.

Miguel loudly cleared his throat into the microphone.

EVERYBODY WANTS TO RULE THE WORLD

Rocky flinched and turned in his seat. A sloppy grin raced across his face.

"You good, bro?" Miguel asked.

"Good?" Rocky threw his arms around his wife's shoulders and pulled her in close. "Bro, I couldn't be better!"

"Fantastic!" Miguel gave the crowd an exaggerated eye roll, which got them laughing once more. "As I was saying… Rocky, you're a complicated man. What you all may not know about us is that the first time Rocky and I met, we almost got into a fight. Yeah, we did. I say *almost*. He was…well, let's just say he was getting a little lippy and someone had to put the oaf in his place." More laughter. "I wish I was joking, but it's the absolute truth, I swear it! Friends tend to meet in the strangest ways, and Rocky and I are no different. I never thought I would be friends with a guy like him, you know? We're both as opposite as can be. I'm short, he's tall. I'm smart, he's dumb. I'm devastatingly handsome, he's…" Even more laughter. "But in all seriousness, despite our initial meeting, despite our differences, I've watched this man over the last fifteen years become a far better person than when we first met. He's worked hard at bettering himself in all facets. I'd like to think the man he is today would look back on his former self and realize what an incredible journey to maturity and adulthood and eventually fatherhood Rocky Saul has taken."

Get near my mother again and I'll fucking kill your black ass! Do you understand me?

Miguel shivered.

"I don't think he could have handled something like marriage even five years ago. But he's a better man these days. He's a changed man. A good man. As a token of your appreciation, I'd like everyone to drop five dollars on this table as a thank you for my services in that regard." Laughter again erupted around the room. Even Rocky was amused, his hands clapping with plastered delight. Miguel grabbed his glass of champagne and raised it high. "Gemma, you have a good one there next to you. Take care of him and keep him in his place—or I'll do it for you!"

With that, the room cheered and downed their drinks.

Miguel beamed with pride. He'd spent months worrying about his speech, knowing it had to be perfect, and now that it was over, he felt nothing but relief. Everyone in the reception hall seemed happy, their smiling faces a warm reminder that better days were ahead. Even the hall workers and the catering crew in the back of the room were clapping as they shuffled around, preparing the banquet dinner.

A large arm suddenly fell over his shoulder. A waft of stale beer breath hit him right in the nose.

"Miguel Toro, ladies and gentlemen!" Rocky yelled drunkenly into the microphone. "Miguel Toro... my brother! I love you, you beaner bastard!"

The room abruptly went quiet. Movement in the back of the hall ceased. Everyone turned to look at them.

Miguel grew cold, his mouth instantly drying. His heart skipped several beats. His stomach sank to his feet. Embarrassment washed over him like a tidal wave.

EVERYBODY WANTS TO RULE THE WORLD

Rocky snatched the microphone from his hand. "What? What did I say?" He glanced at Miguel, then back to the crowd. "What? *Beaner*? You're weirded out because I called him *beaner*? Jesus Christ, it was a joke! A goddamn joke!" Rocky pulled Miguel in closer, nearly choking him with his large forearm. "The guy's my best friend. We rag on each other all the time. Right? I'm not being serious or anything. It's not like I actually mean it. You act like I called him a spic or something, Jesus…"

When he noticed everyone's discomfort, Rocky turned to his wife. She, too, seemed disappointed in his choice of words.

"Oh, give me a fucking break. I didn't… Look, forget I said anything, okay? Let's get the music going, yeah?" He snapped his fingers repeatedly at the DJ in the corner of the room. "Music! Now!"

The DJ pulled a face before pecking at his keyboard. A moment later, Kool and The Gang kicked in over the speaker system, once again filling the room with joyful noise.

His arm still wrapped tight around Miguel, Rocky pulled him in close. "You know I didn't mean anything by that, right?"

Miguel was utterly mortified. He closed his eyes. His fists clenched. Even though the room appeared to be back to normal, he knew everyone still had their minds on *him*. It already took everything in his power to stand up on that stage to give his best man's speech, but to have the groom regretfully insult you in front of the whole room? That made Miguel want to crawl under the table and scream. It was one thing being called slurs in private by friends—hell, it was even one thing to be dubbed it by an angry stranger. But it was a whole *other* thing to be bestowed such careless insults at a crowded party.

Yeah, he knew Rocky didn't mean anything by it. That didn't make it any less hurtful.

Not wanting to make it more awkward, Miguel nodded. "Yeah."

"You good, bro?"

"Yeah."

"You know I love you, right? You know I would never do anything to hurt you?"

Miguel opened his eyes. He glanced sideways at his inebriated friend. "Yeah."

Rocky clapped him on the shoulder. "Good! Now, let's celebrate, baby!" With that, he headed back to his new bride and left Miguel alone at center stage.

An hour rolled past, and Miguel was mostly beginning to feel better. He managed to dance his feelings away, taking his time with each of Gemma's bridesmaids as the wedding party seized the open dance floor. Every face was covered with a smile, every foot shuffling uncoordinated to the beat. By that point in his life, Miguel had been to several weddings, ranging from Puerto Rican to black to white affairs, and nearly all played the same corny song list. But that was just fine. He was feeling good again and was ready to see where the night took him.

After dancing with a little old woman with blue hair, Bridgett, Gemma's maid of honor, slid up to him and put her hands on his waist. Miguel smiled, putting his own hands on her shoulders.

"Hey, there."

EVERYBODY WANTS TO RULE THE WORLD

"Hey yourself," she said, grinning. "Quite the party, yeah?"

Miguel nodded. "You could say that."

Her face grew serious. "You okay?"

"Huh?"

"You know…what Rocky said."

Rolling his eyes, Miguel said. "Oh yeah. That. It's…fine. It's whatever."

Bridgett pursed her lips. "That was really shitty of him. Like, *really* shitty."

"Yeah, well, that's Rocky. What can you do, you know?"

She wasn't buying it. "That shouldn't matter, Miguel. That was an incredibly mean thing he did to you up there. I mean, *I* was embarrassed for you. Like, who does that, you know? Friends or not, that was so ridiculous."

Miguel could only shrug.

She continued. "Look, I know you guys have been real tight for a long time, and I respect that, but… How do you do it?"

"Do what?"

"Stay friends with someone like him?"

Miguel cocked an eyebrow. "How do you mean?"

Sighing, she appeared to choose her words carefully. "Like, you know, he's not the easiest to get along with. I've only known him for a few years now but…I don't know…he just seems hard to get along with. He's such a polar opposite of you. You're so nice and sweet and easy going. He's such a loose cannon. I worry sometimes."

"You worry? About what?"

She shook her head, looking down at the floor. "I don't know. I just worry, you know? About Gemma."

Miguel stared at her worried face. "Bridge, do you know something I don't?"

"No!" she said, immediately shaking her head. "He hasn't done anything. I just… I just worry about what he *can* do. He's a big guy with loads of issues. I know Gemma loves him and all, but…"

Her words hung heavy in the air. Yes, he knew all too well what those issues could amount to. He'd seen it first-hand. He hadn't thought about it before, but suddenly he found himself worrying about things he wasn't supposed to concern himself with.

He finally said, "Look, I wouldn't stress about anything, okay? Sure, he's got his issues, but Gemma has really helped him in so many ways. Trust me, I've seen the way he's changed since she's come into his life. Tonight aside, he's evolved quite a bit. They're both very capable at working on any problems that will come up. And if they can't, I fully expect Gemma to fuck him up."

They both laughed, finally breaking the tension. Bridgett smiled up at him.

"Thank you for your help these last few weeks. You were amazing."

Miguel gave her a nod. "You are very welcome. It was my pleasure." A few moments passed before he finally asked, "Hey, what are you doing later?"

"What do you mean?"

"I mean later, like, after the party is over."

"I don't know. Probably driving back home, I guess."

EVERYBODY WANTS TO RULE THE WORLD

Miguel playfully shrugged. "There's room in my hotel if you wanted to come over tonight."

She offered him a grin. "Miguel Toro, are you hitting on me?"

"That depends… Is it working?"

"*What do you mean they're leaving?*"

Whatever good mood that had accrued had come to an abrupt, screeching halt as Rocky's furious cry echoed throughout the party hall. All at once, every head turned toward the back of the room.

"*Why are they fucking leaving?*"

Miguel sighed. "Jesus Christ…" He then said, "Excuse me," before pushing past Bridgett and working his way toward the quarrel.

By the time he reached Rocky, he knew it was already too late. Red-faced and screaming, Rocky stood before a small Mexican man in a white apron. The man, who Miguel now recognized as the owner of the catering company he helped hire, looked livid himself, but far more composed than the giant, raving groom who towered over him. Hands clenched by his sides, Rocky leaned into the man's face until they were nearly touching noses.

"Explain this horseshit to me one more time, you little twerp! Maybe I somehow misheard your words."

Miguel quickly stepped up beside Rocky and urged him a foot backwards. "Hey, hey, hey! Take it easy, man. Take it easy. What's going on?"

The caterer scowled up at Rocky. "You misheard nothing, *sir*. As I told you several times now, we are leaving."

Rocky ignored Miguel and took a step forward. "*Leaving?* Do you hear this shit? They're fucking leaving!"

Miguel spoke to the caterer. "Sir, may I ask why?"

Behind the caterer, his staff bustled behind the row of folding tables, quickly packing up the food and containers that were already displayed and ready to eat.

The head caterer said, "Because we don't provide our services to racists or their ilk."

Miguel's heart sank.

"*Racist?*" Rocky shouted, throwing his arms up. "You're calling me a fucking *racist*? Why? Because I called my buddy here a *beaner*? Are you fucking *serious* right now? Are you *joking*?"

The man simply shook his head. "This is no joke, sir."

The rest of his staff, most of which were Hispanic, shot looks of disdain their way.

Rocky continued to rant. "Can you believe this *bullshit*? Because I certainly fucking can't!" He jabbed a rigid finger toward the staff. "You dirty little ingrates! You filthy fucking rats! You get back here and put that fucking food back out where it belongs! I paid good money for that goddamn slop you made!"

Miguel felt truly helpless. While his friend was having a full-blown meltdown, the rest of the party observed in horror as the man of the day was making a spectacle out of his careless words. While Rocky's mother was nowhere to be found, Rocky's father and stepmother remained silent off to the side, their faces of disgust more aimed at the caterers than their son. A few people had already left the party, while others were starting to grab their coats and purses. The entire evening was turning out to be a disaster that not even Miguel could save.

"Please, sir," Miguel pleaded. "Is there anything I can do to make this right?"

After stacking the last of the food pans and ordering his staff to wheel out the warming carts to their van, the head caterer turned back to Miguel. Pity wore deep in his exhausted face. "There absolutely *is* something you can do, young man. Get some better friends."

Miguel had nothing to say.

"Naturally, there won't be a refund." With that, he followed his staff out of the building.

Rocky dashed forward and flipped one of the folding tables. "*I'm* a fucking racist? *You're* the fucking racist! What—can't serve a *white* man and his *white* family and friends some goddamn food?"

Gemma ran up beside her husband. "Rocky! Stop this ridiculous nonsense right now!"

He continued to scream, flipping yet another plastic table. "Don't like the word *beaner*, huh? How about *wetback*, you little wetback cocksuckers? Does that suit you better? Get out of my country, you greasy little bastards! Get out or I'll fucking take you out myself!"

"*Rocky Saul!*"

Chest heaving in breathless anger, Rocky ceased his cries and faced his new wife.

"*What the hell is wrong with you?*" she shouted. Tears poured down her face. She glanced about the room in embarrassment, then dashed for the back door.

Rocky hollered, "Gemma! Wait! Come back!" He took off after her.

Miguel found he could not move. He skimmed over the confused eyes of the onlookers and felt nothing but defeat. Bridgett stared at him, her eyes wide, head shaking slowly back and forth.

Maybe the man was right. Maybe Miguel needed better friends.

This is not a coincidence.

While Sue remained by the back wall, trying desperately to get ahold of her boyfriend on their new cell phone, Miguel looked out over the city. He stood with his shoulder against the wall, right at the opening, where the large set of picture windows once were. He normally hated heights, wouldn't even dare to look out the windows of his own office during work hours. The sight had always made him dizzy and nauseous… but what he saw below made him feel both for a very different reason.

In the afternoon daylight, the sun shone through spaces in the sky where they hadn't before. Where there were once high-rises and lumbering apartment buildings, several now had been turned into massive mounds of concrete and steel. Smoke and flames rose like funeral pyres from the rubble. Smaller buildings had been crushed in their wake. Cars and commuter buses buried. Hundreds, if not thousands, of bodies, he imagined, lost. Only in third-world, war-torn countries had Miguel seen this much destruction on such a wide scale. He stared on as those who had left to flee the city zig-zagged through the street-level destruction.

EVERYBODY WANTS TO RULE THE WORLD

Miguel shook uncontrollably. He had been so calm up until then, trying hard to be strong and level-headed for Sue while they attempted to find a way out, but right then, as he watched the city he loved, the place he called home, where he grew up and made his life, reduced to ashes and needless pandemonium, he wasn't sure how to continue on. Physically, he felt disoriented and weak, but mentally... His brain was stuck on repeat.

Why are we still standing? Why aren't we adding to the death toll?

In the distance, more gunshots rang out. Rapid fire hisses blowing in the wind.

No, this is definitely not a coincidence. Something much bigger is happening here.

"Goddamn it!" Sue shouted.

Teary-eyed, Miguel turned toward her. "What's wrong?"

Leaning against the far wall, she repeatedly smashed her fingers against the phone screen. "It died on me. The damn thing went black while I was talking to Gene."

"So, you got through to him?"

"Yes! He wouldn't answer at first because he didn't recognize the number, but he finally picked up."

Miguel wiped his eye. "That's great! Is he okay? Where is he? Is he safe?"

She nodded rapidly. "He and Jean are okay, thank God!" She, too, wiped her eyes, one hand clutching her heaving chest. "He said they were home this morning when the explosions happened. Apparently, they're happening everywhere! All over the country! They had the news on all morning, watching it all. He said there's—Jesus Christ—roving caravans of armed men just…shooting people and taking down police!" She stopped to take a breath, her eyes wide with fright. "Miguel, what's happening out there?"

He shot a quick glance at the hellscape below, before returning his gaze to Sue. "I wish I knew."

"Gene's on his way here."

Miguel stood up straight. "*What?*"

She nodded. "My mother is over at our house right now. She's going to watch Jean while Gene rushes over."

"Sue, that's not a good idea."

"No, no," she said. "The armed men aren't in our neighborhood yet. He's okay to drive here."

"That's not what I mean. I don't think there's anywhere for him to go. It's…not great down there."

"I don't care, Miguel! I don't fucking care! He's on his way right now!"

Swallowing, Miguel stood there in silence, observing Sue as her panic twisted into desperation. She was wholly terrified, and now her partner was traveling across town, braving the conflict to come rescue her. She also had a little girl at home. One Miguel swore he would get Sue back to. Despite his fears and his uncertainty, he wasn't going to break that promise.

Pushing down his trepidation, Miguel stepped away from the window and strode back to his co-worker. She had begun to cry once again, dropping the dead phone to the carpet. Miguel carefully put her arm around his neck and helped lift her up.

"Let's get you home."

She nodded. "Thank you. For everything."

EVERYBODY WANTS TO RULE THE WORLD

"*De nada.*"

Together, they traversed around the debris and smoking human carcasses and headed for the back hallway. The office space was a similar layout to their own, so he switched on the autopilot and moved machine-like past the elevator and through the annex. The annex had taken quite a beating as a separate explosion had nearly destroyed the entire area. Much of the ceiling was gone and now lay about the floor. A dozen or so more bodies had been reduced to cinders, most blown against the walls in the blast. The smell was horrific and strong, choking them the moment they entered the room. Miguel quickly ushered them across the room and around the back corner—

—only to find the entire staircase gone.

Much like the office windows, the entire side of the building was a gaping hole out into the world. Yet another explosion had taken out the stairwell and the wall beyond it. Sunlight welcomed them as they stumbled to a halt. Sue cried out in shock. Miguel felt his heart sink as he cautiously glanced over the lip of the hallway and saw that, much like the opposite stairwell, the stairs were completely impassable. The explosion had taken out the entire wall, and the bracing which kept sections of stairs in place had gone down with it.

There was no way down.

The building shuddered and shook.

Sue screamed, "*What are we going to do?*"

Miguel had no idea, but he *did* know they had to move fast. His brain reminded him of the buildings outside and how they no longer stood upright. They were very much existing on borrowed time.

"Come on."

Turning them around, Miguel moved them back to where they had come from. When they returned to the main office space, the building began to rumble beneath them. Glass jittered on the carpet. Steel and concrete groaned in pain.

Miguel was quickly running out of options. Both staircases were completely impassable. They were still far too high up in the building to even consider jumping an option. He searched the room, trying to will some sort of emergency exit into existence. His heart pounded. Nausea washed over his stomach. Dizziness spun his head. Sue continued to shout and cry.

Outside, gunshots echoed through the air.

There was a roar, then the building rumbled, taking their legs out from under them. Miguel and Sue collapsed to the floor. The sound was tremendous as something above their heads, some upper section of the high-rise, finally broke loose. The massive segment disconnected and slid off the side. A few moments later, the sunlight beyond the window momentarily disappeared as the top of the building fell free to the ground below. When it hit the streets beneath them, an enormous *boom* rocked the building. Miguel threw himself over Sue, shielding her body.

After a few long minutes, the remains of the building had finally ceased shaking. Unlike the high-rise, Miguel had not. He wearily sat up, absolutely convinced that any minute, they would be buried beneath some architect's former dream. But they remained intact.

For now.

EVERYBODY WANTS TO RULE THE WORLD

Sue propped herself on her elbow. "What was that?"

Miguel forced himself to exhale. "A warning."

He glanced over to the elevator doors.

It was all they had left.

Without thinking twice, he stood and then pulled up Sue with him.

"What?" she asked, panicked. "Where are we going?"

He ushered them both to the far side of the office. When they reached the doors, he leaned Sue against the wall next to them.

"The *elevator*? That's your plan? The goddamn elevator?"

Without answering, Miguel attempted to wedge his fingers in-between the two doors, but the thick steel flaps would not budge.

"The power's out, Miguel!" she continued. "You're not going to open it! And you don't even know if the cab is on this floor! You don't know—"

"*I know I don't know!*" he screamed. "*I fucking know I don't know!*" Taking a moment to collect himself, he went on. "Sue…we don't have a choice, okay? This is it. This is all we have left. Now…just let me try this, okay? Please."

Eyes wide with trepidation, she reluctantly nodded.

When he realized his hands weren't enough, he zig-zagged around the office floor, searching for anything he could use to pry open the doors. He sifted through piles of debris, kicking over remains of chairs and desks, nudging aside human remains, but found nothing of use. He needed something thin but strong, something he could wedge deep enough in the crevasse that wouldn't break. Then he found it. He pulled a desk drawer open and spotted a heavy-duty letter opener. The blade was around six inches long and was thin enough for the job.

He raced back over to the doors and stabbed the blade into the crack. When he found he could push it in no further, he gradually leaned into the instrument and pushed sideways. At first, the doors wouldn't budge. The blade began to bend.

The building rumbled once more.

Miguel started to panic.

He pushed in the other direction, straightening the blade once more.

Sue remained silent as she watched him work. But he could feel the anxiety and hope draining from her body.

"Please…" he whispered.

Suddenly, the gap in the door widened. He pushed the blade harder, and the doors responded. Pocketing the letter opener, Miguel wedged his fingers into the slight opening and pulled the door slats in opposite directions.

Almost on their own, the doors slowly slid open. Adrenaline surging, Miguel shouldered them both open the rest of the way.

Sue mumbled, "Son of a bitch…"

Miguel felt his stomach sink.

The elevator shaft yawned before them, but the cab was stuck halfway down between the floors. The cab's doors were open, giving them a view inside.

EVERYBODY WANTS TO RULE THE WORLD

Miguel dropped to his stomach and looked into the four feet of open room they had. The cab itself was empty and dark, but there was a small amount of light at the bottom. Not wanting to lean in too far, he slowly put his head inside and looked below.

The doors on the level below were somehow open.

The building suddenly shuddered—

—the cab jolted and dropped—

—Sue shrieked—

—and Miguel swiftly pulled his head out and scooted backwards.

For a moment, Miguel was convinced the cab was going to plummet down into the building's depths, but the cab remained where it was, only now lower than before. The opening had lessened by nearly a foot.

He glanced up at Sue.

Wide-eyed, she rapidly shook her head. "No! No way in hell!"

"Sue, the doors are open below." He stood and confronted her, putting his hands on her forearms. "Sue!"

In a fit of terror, Sue thrashed her body, attempting to shake him off. "*No! No! There has to be another way! There has to be!*"

"Sue!"

"There has to be—"

"*There isn't another goddamn way!*" Miguel screamed, hating himself in that moment. "*There just isn't!* I know you're scared—hell, I'm scared! I'm so fucking terrified that it makes me sick."

Tears streamed down her face.

He continued. "It's okay to be scared. It's okay. But you're going to have to continue to trust me. You have up until this point, right? Can you continue that?"

Still crying, she nodded, her eyes barely meeting his.

"Good. We're going to get through this. Gene is going to be out there somewhere waiting for us. He may even already be." He pointed toward the elevator. "The sooner we can get down there, the sooner we can get you to him and your daughter. Okay?"

Sue wiped her eyes. "I'm getting really fucking tired of crying."

Miguel gave her a small grin. "You and me both. Hey, at least you have both of your eyes to cry from." Taking her arm around his shoulder, he guided her toward the open elevator door and helped sit her down on her bottom. "Okay, here's what we're going to do. I'm going to send you down first."

"Me first? Why?"

"Because it's going to be easier that way. I don't want you up here by yourself, flipping and contorting and possibly hurting yourself any further. I'm going to help you down into the cab, then I'll be down right after you, then I'll help you up onto the floor below."

"Christ," she moaned, eyeing the cab. "Unless one of us is cut in half, right?"

The thought had crossed his mind, but he urged it away. "Positive thoughts, all right?"

"But what then? So what if we make it through? What do we do then?"

Miguel paused, then said, "One step at a time." With that, he gingerly urged Sue onto her stomach and began to scoot her backwards into the meager opening. Inch by inch she wiggled until all that was left was her upper body. As cautiously as he could, Miguel held onto her wrists until her entire body was dangling inside the cab. His numb hand was starting to regain its feeling, but his grip remained tacky from the dried blood on his fingers and palm.

"Okay, I'm going to lean in and lower you down," he said. "Let me know as soon as you feel the floor."

In the dark below, Sue's tense features stared back up at him. "Not too fast!"

As if on command, the building shuddered hard. The elevator cab screeched, metal on metal, and the cable above them jolted. Miguel panicked and instinctively let go of Sue's hands, throwing himself backwards. Sue screamed and fell into the darkness below. The cab dropped, and for a moment Miguel thought the cab would go away completely. Another foot of opening disappeared as the cab plunged and then stopped. The building continued to quake for a few more moments before eventually petering off.

Miguel crawled back toward the shaft. "Sue! Sue can you hear me?"

Inside the cab, Sue's pained cries met his ears.

"Sue! Speak to me!"

"I…think I broke my leg!" she shouted. "More than before!"

"Shit." He stared at the lack of room in the new opening. "I'm coming down."

Underneath his feet, the floor began to tremor. The wall next to the elevator shaft split, spider webs splintering the drywall and concrete. The cable inside the shaft pulled tight.

Miguel didn't waste any more time. Without thinking twice, he closed his eye and dove head-first into the opening.

He wasn't positive how far the drop was, but he felt as though he was suspended in mid-air for hours. Cold air rushed past his face, cooling the sweat in his brow and his short beard. He could have stayed like that forever. In that moment, he was free from the collapsing building, from the death and the fire and worry. But it didn't last. At some point, his face hit the floor of the cab, breaking his nose on impact. A second later, his body crumpled into a heap. The air instantly exited his lungs. Miguel gagged, trying his hardest to scream. He rolled over and found Sue lying beside him. She squirmed in agony, holding her fractured leg.

When he could finally breathe again, Miguel regarded the open doors of their new floor. It appeared normal and unmarked from the explosion above. He could almost smell the fresh, smokeless air beyond.

"We have to—oh fuck!" He wiped his bloody nose, breathing through his mouth. "Sue, we have to move."

The cab jolted and dropped another foot.

"Sue! Let's go!"

Pushing the pain aside, Miguel sprung to his feet and pulled Sue to hers. She bellowed, her legs buckling beneath her.

Shaking, the cab dropped another few inches and then gradually lowered. The open doorway suddenly revealed itself fully, then began to disappear.

"*Go!*" he barked.

With all his remaining strength, he grabbed Sue around the midsection and tossed her through the remaining opening. Sue rolled, then collapsed to the linoleum floor.

Another foot vanished.

Then another.

Miguel bounded out and quickly pulled himself free from the sinking cab.

A few blinks later, the cab was completely gone.

While Sue writhed in agony, Miguel sluggishly pulled himself up, fresh blood gushing from his nostrils. His knees were like rubber, barely able to hold his weight. He assumed he had given himself a concussion, but there was nothing he could do at that point. They had to keep going, despite their injuries. There was no choice. The building was a ticking time bomb, ready to go down at any minute. Maybe the new floor they were on was fine, but there was no telling what remained beneath their feet.

As if reading his thoughts, the building answered with a fleeting grumble.

"Sue, we have to go."

"I-I can't!" she cried, holding her leg. "I can't get up!"

Taking a deep breath, Miguel delicately lifted her up into his arms. She didn't weigh much, but with his arm still waking up and throbbing, he wouldn't be able to carry her for long. All they had to do was find the other staircases and check their accessibility.

Step by step, Miguel trudged down the barren hallway and past the rows of pristine cubicles and offices until they reached the kitchenette. He shouldered open the door—

—and immediately halted.

Rocky Saul wept over his General Tso's Chicken.

It was a sad sight, to be sure. Pathetic even. Miguel himself wasn't exactly above crying. He enjoyed a good tearjerker movie. He cried when his favorite baseball team won the World Series. Hell, he even wept like a teenage girl when he saw Taylor Swift in concert (not his proudest moment). But this... This was just embarrassing.

The restaurant was mostly quiet, save for the tinny muzak playing over the speakers and the low din of voices from the other tables. It was unusually packed for a Thursday night, but Miguel was happy to see Lin Garden getting the business. There was a time it appeared the restaurant would be closed due to low turnouts, as the much larger Chinese eatery chain across town normally drew away their business. But after several ownership changes and multiple health code violations, the franchise shuttered its doors, and Lin Garden gratefully absorbed their clientele. Miguel was happy for the owner, Bruce, and his wife, Mei. They were good people and deserved their decades of hard work to finally pay off. More than anything, Miguel didn't want to see his favorite local establishment go away. It was close to his apartment and had become his usual first date meet-up when trying to impress whatever new girl he was seeing. Bruce would pull out all the stops for Miguel, preparing the meals himself and decking their table out with the best decorations and dishware he kept stored away for such special occasions.

But tonight, Miguel was just plain mortified to be seen there.

Face red with humiliation, Miguel tried not to peek around as the other patrons side-eyed the large sobbing man sitting directly across from him. It wouldn't have been a big deal if Rocky had just been quietly sobbing to himself. The problem was Rocky never did anything quietly. Bombastic may as well have been his middle name. He blubbered hard, his right hand repeatedly smacking the table, silverware dancing across the tablecloth.

Miguel wasn't sure how or why Rocky started to cry in the first place. Their dinner had started off quietly enough, filled with catching up and frequent awkward silences. The whole night itself was awkward. Miguel never wanted to catch up with Rocky, much less get dinner with him. It had been nearly six years since he'd last seen his former friend in person, and to be perfectly honest, he had hoped it would continue for even longer. It wasn't just the incident at the wedding that ended their friendship. The signs were always there. They couldn't have been clearer. Miguel just chose to overlook them. He'd tried to reason with Rocky, to change and better him in any way he could, but some folks just weren't susceptible to alterations. Rocky was who he was. He always had been, right from the first time they'd met on the school bus. It didn't take a genius to figure out the type of man he would grow up to become. Miguel tried—Lord knows he did—but he eventually had to cut the guy out of his life for good. Not just for his health, but for his sanity. There was only so much intolerance and bigotry one person, especially one of color, could take before they slammed the door shut and locked it. Miguel had spent his entire life living as a Puerto Rican man in a predominantly white country, and no matter what he did, no matter what type of lifestyle he chose to live, he was always treated differently. Not equal. *Different.* The last thing he needed now, as a man in his thirties, was to be close to someone who solidified those divergences. After years of obtuse negativity, Miguel craved optimism and progressive thinking. Upbeat attitudes and creative adventures. Small mindedness and chaotic narcissism would always be the downfall of someone like Rocky Saul. Miguel Toro refused to be brought down by it any longer.

What he couldn't continue to ignore were Rocky's incessant attempts to reconcile. Miguel hadn't changed his phone number, but he thought about it fairly regularly. The first year after calling their friendship quits, Rocky would buzz him at least once a week. Miguel would always ignore it, but that didn't stop the other man from trying. He would leave voicemails ranging from long, tedious stories about his week to spiteful rants over why they were no longer companions. Every message would end with a promise that he was doing better, that he was trying harder—"So, so hard, you don't even know!"—to be a better person. Miguel appreciated his intentions, but he knew they were for naught. He didn't need the drama, so he never answered the calls.

EVERYBODY WANTS TO RULE THE WORLD

The calls eventually started to drop off until they went away all together. Miguel was glad. He had finally started to feel normal for the first time in decades, wasn't having to worry about the ticking time bomb standing next to him. He started to date more, travel more, experience more. All of his past worries seemed to drift away. But they weren't completely gone. Somewhere deep in the back of his mind, he still worried about Rocky Saul. Despite his newfound lease on life, a little part of him hoped his former friend truly *was* striving to change himself. Maybe this break-up was the best thing for Rocky. Maybe it made him realize he had to change his thoughtless, bigoted ways in order to exist in an ever-changing world. What happened at his wedding, for better or worse, may have been the catalyst for his hard reset. But who really knew? Miguel refused to keep up with Rocky and what his personal life had become over the last several years. As far as he knew, he was still married to Gemma, and from what he heard from a friend of a friend, they had a little boy. He sincerely hoped that child had a good man raising him.

By the time Miguel had received the email, he had nearly forgotten about Rocky Saul altogether. It had almost been deleted, but he decided to open it and discovered who the message was from. Miguel sat at his desk at work, staring at his phone, shocked at who was reaching out. The email was simple, wanting to know how Miguel was and hoping he and his family were doing okay. What really stuck out was the lack of eagerness. There were no pleas for forgiveness, no begging to see things his way. It was merely a simple catching up between two old friends.

The email ended with Rocky suggesting they maybe get together and have dinner sometime soon. Nothing more than that. Miguel sat on the email for nearly a week, the handful of modest lines running through his brain on repeat. Perhaps Rocky Saul had changed? Maybe it was boredom or maybe it was curiosity that got the better of him, but he eventually wrote back and agreed to grab some food with his old friend. Just food and conversation. Nothing more.

He was already regretting his decision.

When Rocky was halfway through his plate of glazed chicken bites, he began to only look down at his food. He then stopped eating altogether and dropped his fork.

Miguel, his mouth full of creamy pork, stared at his former friend. "Rock?"

That's when the bigger man started to cry. His chest hitched, his lower lip curling out like a pouty child. A shrill whine escaped his throat, then a full burst of sobs detonated behind it.

Unsure what to do, Miguel watched as Rocky's weeping grew louder and louder. Soon, everyone in the restaurant, patrons and staff alike, were watching. Miguel wanted to sink down in his seat and disappear. He wasn't embarrassed that Rocky was crying, per se—men and women were allowed to show emotion as they pleased. It was the implication of what was coming next. He fully expected Rocky to loudly beg for Miguel's forgiveness, to take him back as his friend, that he missed him and relished what they used to have. It truly didn't surprise him Rocky would have waited until they were in public to do this. Everything the man did, for as long as Miguel had known him, was loud and audacious.

What Miguel wasn't expecting was what Rocky *really* had to say.

"She's gone, man…"

Miguel pulled a face. "What?"

"She's fucking gone, man. Gone!"

"Gone? What do you mean? Who—Gemma?"

Rocky pounded the table with his fist, nearly toppling their drinks. "Who do you think, man? Of course Gemma!"

"Jesus Christ, Rocky… I'm so sorry."

He waved Miguel off. "She's not dead. She fucking left me!"

Miguel finally relaxed. Though he was no longer on a regular speaking basis with Rocky, he still cared for Gemma. He spent so much time with the two of them before they were married, and though he always felt like the third wheel, he greatly enjoyed her company. She was a warm, sweet, delicate person, who often made Miguel laugh harder than many others could. She was the complete opposite of her husband in every way, which made their attraction to one another so peculiar. Then again, so was he and Rocky's friendship. He would never say it out loud, but he gleefully thought, *Good for her.*

"I'm sorry to hear that, Rock," Miguel finally offered. "I really am."

Rocky growled and punched his plate of food. Chunks of poultry and white rice flew through the air and landed *splat* across the table. The plate shattered into several pieces.

Eyes dripping with emotion, Rocky glanced around the room, finding all the confused eyes were on him. "What the fuck are you all looking at? Mind your goddamn business!"

From the back room, Bruce strode out toward their table. Miguel immediately put his hand up, letting him know he had this under control. Bruce scowled and shook his head, staying put.

Miguel turned back to Rocky. "You need to calm down, man. Calm the hell down."

"How can I calm down," Rocky yelled, "when all these deadbeats are staring at me like some sideshow freak? Is my fucking misery amusing to you all? Huh? Want me to get up and dance for you all like a little monkey with an organ?"

"Rocky!"

"You fucking schmucks! You fucking losers!"

Miguel slammed the table with his palm. "*Enough!*"

Huffing, Rocky finally stopped ranting. He turned toward Miguel, his eyes wide with fear.

"If you don't calm yourself," Miguel continued, lowering his voice to a growl, "I'm going to pay for my food and walk right out. Right the fuck out. You feel me? I will leave this place, and I will absolutely never speak another word to you. Do you understand?"

Swallowing, Rocky gave him a slight nod.

For the first time that evening, Miguel really looked at Rocky. Over the last several years, the man had put on some weight. It didn't really show in his face, but his gut suggested many of his daily meals were replaced by alcoholic beverages. His hair was rapidly vanishing, the remaining strands now an endangered species. Rocky had normally kept a clean-shaven face, but the thick mustache on his upper lip gave him the appearance of someone fifteen years older. Even his clothes were ill-fitting and dirty, like he had stopped taking care of himself as a whole. Truth be told, he looked like complete shit.

"Good. Now…start from the beginning. Calmly, please."

Rocky glanced down at his bleeding hand, then back up at Miguel. "Like I said, Miggy. Gemma…she walked out on me. Left me like I wasn't shit."

"When did this happen?"

"Two months ago."

"What happened?"

Rocky shrugged. "I don't know, man. I really don't. I thought…" He began to cry again but quickly shook his head, as if pushing it away. "I thought we were doing okay, you know? Sure, we've had our ups and downs. Who doesn't? Nobody's perfect. I'm not, she's not. You're certainly not."

Miguel forced himself not to get up and leave.

"Ever since that…incident…at the wedding, she and I haven't really been the same. It's like no matter what I did or said, there was always tension between us. Resentment. Do you know what it's like to have to live life walking on eggshells?"

"All too well."

"I honestly thought having little Matty would help change things, you know? But it didn't. She spent all her time doting on him, and I felt like I'd been left behind in the dust. Don't get me wrong, Miggy. I love my son. I adore that little shit with all my heart, but goddamn, a man can only take so many cold shoulders before enough is enough." His eyes grew distant and glassy. "I've spent the last several years trying to better myself. Honest, man. I've kept my job, food on the table, a roof over their heads, clothes on their backs. Took them on expensive vacations. Hell, I even paid for Gemma's new tits, not that she ever let me see them. Two grand for a pair of headlights she only let me touch once. Ain't that some shit?"

Miguel was rapidly losing his patience. "What did you do, Rock?"

Rocky eyed him. A small grin appeared on his face. "You always cut to the chase, don't you? I miss that, man. Okay, yeah. Like I said, Gemma and I, we haven't been all that…intimate for a long time. A *long* time. I guess you can deduce I started seeing someone. It wasn't supposed to last. We met online on one of those hook-up apps and were only supposed to see each other a couple of times, but…a couple of times somehow became a couple of years."

Miguel rolled his eyes. "For fuck's sake, man."

"I know, I know. I can hear your thoughts. I know what you're thinking of me. It's nothing I haven't already said about myself. I did what I did, and I'm not proud of it. But I had to, Miggy. I *had* to. I was going crazy. You don't know what it's like to have your woman not want to touch you or be sexual with you. It's absolute hell. You're lucky. You've always been a free man. You haven't had to deal with this same bullshit. I envy you, man."

"All right." Miguel had heard enough. He pushed his chair back to stand.

"No, no, no!" Rocky blurted. "Please! I'm sorry! I shouldn't have said that. You're right. I'm a dickhead. I'm sorry. My apologies."

Miguel slowly sat back down. "Get on with the story, Rock."

"Yeah, yeah. So…yeah. Gemma obviously found out. I thought I was being careful hiding it all. Hell, two years is a long time to keep something like that a secret, you know? She went through my phone one night after I fell asleep, and she found some pics of Lucy and I in my camera roll. I knew I should have hidden them or deleted them or whatever…but I couldn't. I just couldn't. I wanted proof I could make a woman happy. I needed to be able to see that whenever I was feeling down."

"So, then she left you?"

The dam broke once more as fat tears cascaded down Rocky's cheeks. "And she took Matty with her. She took my son away from me, man. My own flesh and blood! I love that kid with every ounce of my soul. I love him more than myself, Miggy!"

"Is she going to let you see him?"

"I don't know! She won't even see me in person. She only calls me maybe once a week on the phone to relay any information she has from her divorce lawyer. It's a fucking joke, man. She refuses to let me see my own child." His voice got louder, shriller. "I miss him so goddamn much, Miggy! I don't know how much longer I can be without him!"

Miguel tried to shush him. "I understand, Rock. I get it."

"No, you don't, man! That ain't even the worst of it!"

"What else happened?"

Rocky threw his hands up in frustration. "On top of it all, I lost my job! There had been rumors of downsizing at the plant, but we all just ignored it. Every manufacturing facility hears shit like that, you know? But three weeks ago, they announced they were shutting down operations at the end of the month and moving all the work to India. Fucking *India*! Good, honest, hardworking Americans losing their long-standing jobs for what? Some Punjabi fuckers to undercut and take our work right out from under us? Unbelievable!"

Gritting his teeth, Miguel sneered, "You're right, Rock. You sure do sound like a changed man."

"Look, I'm sorry, man! I can't help it this time. I busted my ass for ten fucking years at that place. I moved up to engineer and was working my way up to management when this happened. I have every right to be pissed off. And you know what the kicker is? They actually had the balls to ask if I wanted to keep my position and transfer to fucking Mumbai. Give me a break. I told them to shove it up their cheap, penny-pinching asses, and I quit. You understand where I'm coming from, right? This isn't me being *intolerant* or whatever. This is me being rightfully irate they took my livelihood away. They took my life away, man!"

Closing his eyes, Miguel sluggishly rubbed his face with his shaking hands. He wanted to scream. He wanted to stand up and run away from this pathetic excuse of a man. It had been years since he decided to wash his hands of the boat anchor that was Rocky

Saul, to rid himself of the negativity and abject hate this man felt for anyone who wasn't *him*. None of this entire conversation was doing his fear of slipping backwards in time any favors, and yet…here he was…feeling *sorry* for his former friend. He felt pity. He felt shame.

He desperately wished he felt nothing.

"I don't know what to do with myself, Miggy," Rocky whined. "I just don't know. I have to get my wife and child back. I have to prove to them that I'm not some piece of shit degenerate cheater. I don't want my lapse in judgement to define the rest of my life, man. I already lost my job. I can't lose them too. I'm already going to have to sell my damn house. I just… I don't know where to begin. I can't seem to find work anywhere. No one is hiring around here. If I can get a new job and prove to Gemma I can take care of myself, then maybe she'll reconsider."

Miguel sighed long and hard. He stared blankly at the broken, downtrodden man across the table, wanting to let him wallow in his misfortune. He'd caused pain to countless others, and yet, like so many men before him, it all came back around tenfold. This was where Miguel should have lightly patted Rocky on the shoulder, paid for dinner, and then headed home for a good night's sleep. He didn't owe this man a single thing. He had moved on so long ago…

…and yet…

"If you want, Rock, I can see if any of the firms inside my office building are hiring?"

Miguel froze just inside the door frame.

His breath caught in his throat.

The sizeable man hunched over at the sink quickly stood up and spun around to face them. While half of his face was covered with a wet, dripping dish towel, his exposed eye was wide with shock. His dark green army jacket and jeans were mostly burned and covered in charred holes, the small kitchen permeating with the stench of smoke and burnt hair.

"*Rocky?*"

Ten steps away, Rocky Saul stared at them in silence. For several long seconds, nobody spoke a word. Miguel's heart pounded, his thoughts running a mile a minute.

After what felt like an eternity, Rocky finally uttered, "Help me…" before collapsing to his knees.

His elation blinding him, Miguel nearly forgot he was carrying Sue. He stumbled forward until they reached Rocky, and they both collapsed to the floor in front of him. Sue yelped as she hit the ground, groaning in pain. The letter opener in Miguel's pocket stabbed him uncomfortably in the thigh.

"Rocky!" Miguel shouted, grabbing the other man's shoulders. "Holy shit, man! You're here! You're alive!"

Sue asked, "Who is this? You know him?"

"Yes, he's…" *My friend*, he thought. Hands gripping him tight, Miguel gawked at Rocky as the other man propped his back against the cabinets below the sink. Rocky was seriously injured. His clothing had been badly scorched, as was the skin on his neck and face. The hair on one side of his head had been singed to his scalp. What little skin that hadn't been blackened had already grown bright red and angry with welts. The burns were bad and would certainly leave heaps of nasty scars, but they were nothing he would die from, at least not with the proper medical attention.

Miguel found it hard to breathe.

My friend. I helped him get this job…and he nearly died…because of me. He wouldn't be here if it wasn't for me.

Miguel's eye grew wet. "I can't believe—you're here! You're alive! How?"

Rocky's wide eye stared in disbelief. "*You're* here?"

Miguel laughed out of sheer exasperation. "Saturday's a workday, buddy."

Rocky could only nod. Miguel realized the other man was very much in shock. Though his arm was regaining its mobility, Miguel was still in a great deal of disregarded pain, but he was fortunate to avoid getting burned. Even the fall onto his face paled in comparison. This close, Miguel could feel the unnatural warmth of Rocky's scalded flesh, could sense the tenderness beneath his fingers.

He now had *two* other lives in his hands.

"It… It hurts…" Rocky moaned through gritted his teeth.

"I know, brother. I know. We're all three messed up." Blood dripped into Miguel's mouth from his broken nose, which he turned his head and spat out. His two front teeth wiggled loosely against his tongue.

"My…face."

"I know, man. How bad is it?"

Rocky sluggishly shook his head. "I don't know. I can't…feel it."

"Can I look?" When Rocky nodded, Miguel reached out and carefully lifted the wet towel. He immediately cringed.

The skin beneath was already swelling up and leaking a clear pus. The burn covered nearly half of Rocky's face, reaching from his ear to just past his nose. His eyelid was nearly gone, and his eye beneath was completely grayed, the pupil all but wiped out. His lip had been curled by the heat, a small number of yellowed teeth now exposed.

Miguel moaned, "Oh…Jesus, man."

"Bad?"

"Just… Just keep the cold rag on it for now." A sob wound up Miguel's throat. "I'm so sorry, man. God damn, I'm so sorry."

Rocky only gazed back, breathing heavily.

The building tremored once more.

Sue finally spoke up. "Guys, listen. This is sweet and all, but we can't keep sitting here. We have to keep moving, yeah?"

Miguel wiped his eye and nodded. "Yeah. Yeah, you're absolutely right. I don't think we have much time, man. The building has taken too much damage. It feels like the whole thing is ready to come down any minute. Come on."

After standing with a grunt, Miguel carefully pulled Sue back up, apologizing for dropping her, then helped Rocky up to his feet. Despite the agony he was clearly in, he appeared in good enough shape to walk on his own. Sue was not as fortunate. The fall in the elevator had broken her leg, and now her ankle was rapidly swelling. Her dark skin had ballooned to twice its normal size, rendering her right leg completely useless.

"Can you help me carry Sue?" Miguel asked Rocky. "The more help I can get with her, the faster we can move."

Rocky eyed them both, his gaze lingering on Sue. After a few moments, he nodded. "Yeah, I can do that."

Together, they each took an arm and easily held Sue's leg off the floor. "Thank you," she said to Rocky.

Rocky didn't respond.

All together, Miguel led them swiftly through the kitchenette and into a back hallway. The problem was he really had no idea where to go from there. This particular floor space had been designed much different than the last few, the layout and room placements unfamiliar, so he was now only moving by impulse. He steered them down multiple rows of tightly-packed cubicles and storage closets full of computer servers, which blinked and whirred behind glass windows. Somehow, this bottom half of the building still had some power to it.

"Where are we going?" Rocky asked in a drowsy voice.

Sue answered through gritted teeth, "My partner is on his way to pick us up. He might even be down there right now, waiting."

Rocky shook his head. "I don't think that's possible. The streets are nearly unpassable."

"What?"

"Yeah… I think some more of those explosions happened on the lower levels. And when the building's top came down…"

Sue unexpectedly became frantic. "I don't understand. Why are you saying that? What do you mean?"

"I'm saying…I don't think he's coming."

"Of course he's coming! Why the hell do you keep saying that?"

Miguel said, "Guys, come on. This isn't doing us any damn good. I'm sure he's down there right now. Let's keep moving."

Rocky huffed but didn't speak.

Miguel kept them progressing until they reached a long, narrow hallway. At the end of the hall, a glowing red EXIT sign stood out like a heavenly beacon.

Rocky immediately stopped them. "No good."

"What do you mean?" Miguel asked.

"The stairs are out."

"The stairs are out? Like, they're gone?"

"Yeah."

"Are you sure?" Miguel pushed to move them ahead anyways. "Those are the emergency stairs. We were on them not that long ago before we had to cut across. We should at least check—"

Rocky hastily pulled the three of them back. "No, no, no. Trust me. The stairs are out."

"Then why the hell did you let me lead us back here if you knew they were inaccessible?"

Rocky pointed down another smaller side hallway. "The other elevator."

Both Sue and Miguel pulled a face. "The *other* elevator?" he asked. "What are you talking about?"

The other man simply shrugged. "The executive elevator? I thought you knew about it?"

"Why the hell would I know about that, Rock?"

"It goes all the way to every floor. I mean, it's only accessible to a few higher-ups, so I guess not everyone knows about it. Mostly the bosses use it. Sometimes maintenance or cleaning staff."

Miguel instantly felt sick. He had no idea there was *another* elevator in the building they could have used. His mind darted through his former office space, searching through every usable room, and he couldn't think of where that second elevator door could have been.

"I think I saw ours once," Sue said. "It's on the other side of the breakroom, back in the annex by the storage closet. I saw it during orientation."

Miguel shook his head in frustration. "Well shit. Let's go check it out."

After a brisk shuffle down the dark corridor, they came to a small door in the wall that looked more like a sliding closet flap than an elevator opening. Rocky pulled out a set of keys and stuck one in the keyhole next to the door. A small red light above the door lit up, and a moment later, the door slid open and revealed a dimly lit cab.

"I'll be damned," Miguel mumbled as they piled in.

Rocky hit the first-floor button, and the door whisked shut. The cab groaned to life as they commenced to descend.

For the first time in hours, Miguel finally experienced a small sense of relief. The knot in his stomach had begun to uncoil, and the constant wave of nausea was already fading away. He closed his eye and inhaled deeply, letting his weary exhale gradually through his nose. They weren't out of the woods yet, but the sunlight was coming in through the trees, lighting their way home.

Miguel opened his eye and watched Rocky, who had let go of Sue and was now leaning against the opposite wall. The uncovered half of his face grimaced in pain. "I'm so sorry, Rock."

Rocky didn't move his head as he glanced over. "What for?"

"For…this. All of this. I'm sorry you had to go through this. If it wasn't for me, you wouldn't have been here. You wouldn't be hurt."

Once again, Rocky only answered with a shrug.

He must still be in shock, Miguel thought. *The pain hasn't hit him fully yet.*

Miguel continued, "Listen, man… I'm really sorry about what happened between us—"

Rocky immediately waved him off. "Don't. It's fine."

"No, it's not. We could have died today, man. Hell, we still can. I just… I feel responsible for you being here."

"Miguel, stop."

"I just wish I knew what was happening, you know? Like, who was setting *explosives* off—and why? Sue's partner said there's, like, armed militia gunning people down in the streets. Apparently it's happening all over the country! Is this event related to that? I mean… what's happening out there?"

Sue added, "Crazy assholes out there murdering innocent people. Slaying them in cold blood." She shook her head, scowling. "They better stay away from my baby, or I swear to God…"

"I have no doubt she's in good hands right now." Miguel squeezed her shoulder. "She sounds like a tough kid."

"She is." Sue broke down once more, her chest hitching with heavy sobs. "What is this fucking world coming to? I don't want to raise my child in a country like this. What is *wrong* with everyone? Why are people so terrible? Why can't we be free of hate and fear?"

Rocky muttered, "Maybe that's what they're fighting for."

The elevator jolted hard. Miguel felt his feet go out from under him, and for a few seconds, he was suspended in midair. He heard Sue scream, and then the three of them crumpled into a crowded heap on the floorboard. Something clattered across the tight space and landed near Miguel.

Sue shrieked, "*My leg! Oh God!*"

Feeling sick all over again, Miguel held is head, warding off his concussive dizziness. Somewhere above them, the elevator cables screeched loudly into the hollow shaft. The lights inside the cab blinked rapidly before thankfully staying on. Another minor jolt, and the cab began to properly lower.

Sue continued to bellow in pain. Beside them, Rocky held his face. Blood spread across the rag and dripped down his chin and neck. He got up to his knees, steadying himself on the wood paneled wall.

When the dizziness passed, Miguel tried to help Sue upright. "*No!*" she shouted, sweat gleaming on her face. "If it wasn't broken before…it definitely is now! Son of a fucking bitch!"

Rocky tapped on his coat, rubbing his reddened hands over his pockets. He turned his head, searching the floor beneath him.

"Rock, help me with Sue." He noticed on the main panel they were getting close to the bottom floor. A flutter of excitement buzzed through his body.

"Shit, where is it?" Rocky's actions had grown frantic. He quickly stood and spun in place.

"Where's what? Come on, man. Help us out!"

Rocky shouted, "Mother fucker!" Using both hands, he patted his jacket, then moved to his pants. The blood-soaked rag fell away from his face, revealing the upsetting damage underneath. "No, no, no…"

"Dude! What's the matter with you?" Miguel moved to his knees, sitting Sue's back against the wall. "What are you looking for?"

When Miguel shifted his foot, something slid on the floor behind him. He leaned back and reached for the small item.

A chilling numbness spider-walked across Miguel's arms, working its way through his extremities and creeping down into his thudding heart. His mouth instantly went dry. A tinnitus-like buzz started up in his ears.

The device in his shaking hands was about seven inches long and appeared to be entirely homemade. Across its black, sheet metal surface, several small light-switch-like triggers had been haphazardly soldered and screwed together side-by-side along the top of the rectangular box. Four of the triggers—two on one end, one in the middle, and another on the opposite side—appeared to have been flipped, while the other six remained in the down position. A short spiral antenna had been built to retract from the end.

Above him, Rocky's gaze found Miguel's hands.

Sue asked through gritted teeth, "What's that?"

Miguel's eye lifted to meet his friend's.

Rocky's face contorted into a myriad of emotions and empty declarations he couldn't quite express. His lips moved silently, thoughts unable to form into solid words. He finally shook his head and sighed.

"I didn't know you were working today."

Miguel's lips trembled. "Rock… What did you do?"

Sue stared at the device. "Is that…?"

Frowning, Rocky closed his only usable eye. "You wouldn't understand, Miggy."

"I…wouldn't understand? *I wouldn't understand?* What the *fuck* do you mean I wouldn't *understand?*"

"Miggy, lower your—"

Miguel exploded. "*Don't fucking tell me to lower my voice!*"

Rocky threw his hands up in defense.

Arms shaking, the remote trigger felt as heavy as a concrete brick. He wanted to drop it or throw it as hard as he could to get it away from his person. Yet…he couldn't let it go. The item in his palms, this homemade detonator, had already taken hundreds of lives. Needless deaths. Countless devastated families. Pillows without heads to hold. Partners without lips to kiss. Children without warmth to comfort them.

All with the flick of a trigger.

It was that easy.

And Rocky Saul was the one who hit the switches.

I just feel responsible for you being here…

…and now he was responsible for all of their casualties.

All of them.

Miguel breathlessly asked, "Why? Make me understand."

Wiping the blood from his face with his hands, Rocky shook his head and sighed. "This would have happened with or without you, man. If it didn't happen here, it would have happened elsewhere."

"I don't—"

"Look, man, I get it. You're freaked out. That's completely understandable. We've all been through a lot today. Why don't you just hand that over, and we can have a rational conversation about all of this."

Miguel scowled. "Not a chance."

Reaching behind his back, Rocky produced a pistol, which he immediately pointed at Miguel. "I'm not going to ask again, Miggy."

Sue screamed and backed herself up into the opposite corner.

"Are you going to shoot me?" Miguel asked, his chin up. "Then fucking shoot me. Because this thing no longer belongs to you."

Rocky rolled his eye. "How brave of you." He quickly stepped forward and swung the pistol at Miguel's head, cracking him across the cheek. Rocky then grabbed the remote from his grasp and took a step back.

Miguel collapsed to the floor with a huff. Blood dribbled down his face, his already swollen features throbbing. Sue grasped at him and tried to pull him back.

EVERYBODY WANTS TO RULE THE WORLD

"Look what you made me do, man!" Rocky shouted. "I didn't want to fucking do that, but you wouldn't listen!"

Miguel growled, "Screw you, redneck!"

The elevator came to a relaxed halt, and the door to their right leisurely slid open.

"Get the fuck out," Rocky ordered, using his gun like an extended finger. "*Now!*"

Miguel defiantly stood and carefully helped Sue up on to her good leg. She spat at Rocky. "You fucking pig!"

They prudently exited the elevator, followed by Rocky, who never lowered the gun. They found themselves finally back on the ground floor, the end of their horrific journey, but Miguel didn't feel the relief he'd been optimistically searching for. Just down the hallway was the main lobby. From where they stood, he could see the front windows and the overcast sky beyond. He feared in that moment, he had already seen his last sunny day.

"*Screw you, Rocky*," the other man mocked. "*You fucking pig!* You both think I haven't heard that and *so* much worse my entire fucking life? Originality was never your strong suit, Miggy."

"*Originality?*" Miguel hissed. "You're one to talk, you walking stereotype! Angry white man doesn't get his way and decides to kill everyone around him because he's inadequate in every possible sense. Sound about right, Rocky? Did I miss anything?"

"You don't fucking understand me! You never did! You always judged me and made me feel like I was some piece of shit for feeling the way I did about things."

"That's because you *are* a piece of shit!" Miguel screamed. "You've always been that way. I chose to overlook it for years. Hell, I even tried to help you change, but you absolutely refused!"

"*Stop calling me that!*" Rocky's roar echoed throughout the barren hallway. "We may have been best friends, but you never *actually* got to know me, Miggy. You never *understood* me. Never even tried. My father used to beat me regularly! Did you know that? And when my mother ran off with that nigger, those beatings got worse! I thought getting older and getting a job and wife and kid would change that—but guess what? It fucking didn't! Everything got worse, man! They took my job, my wife, my son! They took *everything* from me! *Everything!* And all you can do is stand there and *judge* me?"

Miguel let a few heartbeats pass before he spoke again. "You know what that's called, Rocky? Do you know what everything you just said is *actually* called? It's called *life*. Everybody goes through shit like that, to one degree or another, you fucking idiot! But do you know what ninety-nine percent of people *don't* do? They don't murder innocent people over their heartbreaks!"

Rocky croaked out a dry laugh. "Innocent… Who are you to say who's innocent or not? There goes Miguel Toro, always judging people without actually understanding them."

"Yep, that's me, Rocky. Nail on the head."

"Do you want to know who *doesn't* judge me? Who accepts me for exactly who I am? My new brothers in the TSOA."

"The *who?*"

100

EVERYBODY WANTS TO RULE THE WORLD

"The True Sons of America. You've already met them today. Well, heard them anyways. Listen."

They all three grew quiet. Outside the building, gunfire continued to ring out in the distance. Each *pop* was an exclamation to Rocky's illogical point.

"You joined a terrorist group?"

Rocky shook his head. "Of *course* you'd call us terrorists. Once again, your originality is showing. We're liberators, Miguel. Cultural emancipators. Since the government can't be bothered these days to take the necessary measures to do what's *right* for this country, we've taken it upon ourselves to do it for them."

"What does that even mean?" Sue asked, panic wavering her voice. "That you're rising up and killing minorities and anyone you don't like? You racist fucking scumbag!"

"Yes, bitch. Among many other things."

"You're never going to get away with this!"

Rocky turned the pistol toward her. "Keep talking and you're absolutely going to be next."

Sue went to retort, but Miguel spoke first. "How long, man? How long have you been a part of this bullshit alliance?"

Rocky focused his attention back to Miguel but left the gun pointing at her. "A few years now. Enough to know it should have been a hell of a lot longer."

"I'm still struggling to figure this whole thing out. Why blow this building up? Why kill all these people?"

"As you can see," Rocky said, pointing to his marred face, "this didn't go quite according to plan. I've got explosives rigged on every couple of floors. I was supposed to detonate all of them at the exact same time after I got out of the building, just like the others around the city, all at the same exact time. But as I was performing my run-through, a few of these triggers accidentally flipped in my pocket—"

"And you almost killed yourself in the process," Miguel finished. "Well done. Once again, you still can't get anything right."

Rocky scowled and lifted the remote, shaking it. "Oh, don't worry. This building is still rigged. All I have to do is hit the rest of them and London Bridge comes tumbling down."

Miguel glared hard at the man across from him. He'd known him for nearly his entire life, for as long as his memory could go back, and yet this person—this symbolic figure—was now a complete stranger to him. He may have looked the same and spoke in a familiar cadence, but whatever version of Rocky Saul he used to call his friend had been replaced by an unrecognizable monster. Miguel desperately wanted to find something to appeal to, some little bit of that unmanageable kid he used to hang out with, that unwieldy teenager he cruised the backroads with, or that downtrodden adult he leaned on in hard times…but none of that person was left. What remained in his place could not be reasoned with. Could not be bargained with or appealed to.

Miguel was completely out of options.

"So, what now, Rocky? Where do we go from here?"

Standing five feet away, Rocky Saul studied Miguel like he was an animal in a cage. Miguel's skin crawled.

EVERYBODY WANTS TO RULE THE WORLD

Rocky finally answered, "Come with me."

"*Excuse me?*"

"You heard me. Come with me. Join us. We're millions strong. We can use a fighter like you in our ranks. I'll vouch for you, man, no problem."

Miguel couldn't stop himself. A giggle wound up his throat and quickly evolved into a full bout of uncontrollable cackling. Beside him, Sue gawped at Miguel like he'd lost his mind. Rocky, on the other hand, immediately formed a frown.

When Miguel finally caught his breath, he said, "I'd rather die than ever fucking join your white supremacist terrorist group."

For a long time, Rocky didn't speak. He glowered hard at Miguel, his eye burning holes right through him.

Eventually Rocky muttered, "Remember…this was your decision."

The gun went off in his hand.

The blast reverberated throughout the hallway.

Sue screamed and dropped to the floor.

A moment later, Miguel joined her.

The pain was immediate and all consuming. A red-hot fire exploded in his guts, setting everything inside of his stomach ablaze. Miguel gasped for air, his ears ringing, eye full of stars.

Sue screamed long and hard. With all her strength, she scooted backwards until she was completely out of arm's reach. "*Miguel! No! You shot him, you bastard! You fucking shot him!*"

"And you're next, you loud-mouthed cunt!" He turned his attention back to Miguel, who was writhing in breathless agony. Blood ran from the wound in his stomach and pattered the linoleum floor beneath him. Rocky's eye grew wet. "Goddamn it. *Goddamn it, man!* Look what you made me do! *You* made me do this! We could have *been* something, Miggy! We could have done something *special* together with this group! You were like a brother to me, man." He wiped his face with the back of his pistol hand. "I loved you, bro. Well done, man. Well fucking done! Bravo!"

Outside, just beyond the front windows, a car horn began to beep. Once, twice, then one long blast.

Sue turned to look. *"Gene! Gene, I'm here!"*

"You're not going anywhere!" Rocky barked. "All you people are the fucking same. Thinking you're always going to get your way. This is the new America, sweetheart. The True Sons are in charge now. What *we* say goes. And Simon says know your fucking role and sit still!"

Sue refused to listen. With all her strength, she awkwardly climbed up onto her one good leg and, leaning against the wall, began to hop towards the lobby.

"Get back here, you fucking whore!" Rocky finally left his spot and started off toward her.

Sue screamed and pushed herself harder.

Rocky strode toward her, his gun out.

Sue lost her balance and hit the floor with a hard *thump.*

"No! Leave me alone! Stop! Go away!"

As soon as Rocky stepped past Miguel's prone form, Miguel quickly extracted the letter opener from his pants pocket. He then rolled over onto his side and swung the blade down, sinking it deep into Rocky's calf.

EVERYBODY WANTS TO RULE THE WORLD

Rocky squealed in pain and dropped to his knees. Taking the letter opener handle with both hands, Miguel drug the dull blade down as hard as he could, opening a foot long length of flesh to the world. Bright arcs of blood spat across the floor, spraying all over Miguel's hands and arms. Howling in agony, Rocky collapsed to his stomach, his arms splayed out before him. Miguel then lifted the dull blade and drove it down into the center of Rocky's back, just below the shoulder blades. The man gasped for air, his legs kicking out beneath him.

Several feet away, Sue clumsily got back up to her feet. *"Miguel!"*

Leaning on Rocky's back, Miguel waved her on. "Go! Get to Gene!"

Sue wept. "Not without you! I can't leave you behind!"

Miguel shook his head, his own tears blurring his vision. "Go, Sue. Get to your daughter. Give her a hug for me, okay?"

Sue looked as though she were going to move his way, but the car horn outside called out, breaking her forward motion. She glanced backwards, then back at Miguel.

"Thank you."

Miguel nodded, then watched as she carefully hopped down the hallway and out of sight. Eventually he heard the front door open and then slam close.

The pain in his stomach abruptly returned, and Miguel could ignore it no longer. Screaming, he rolled off of Rocky's body, and with every ounce of energy he had left, he extracted the blade and rolled his old friend over on his back.

Gasping for breath, Rocky stared up at Miguel with a bloodshot eye. "I…" he gasped, struggling for air, "I don't want…to die…"

Miguel snatched the remote from Rocky's loose grip and collapsed onto his own back. "They didn't get that choice. Neither do you."

Rocky cried, "*No!*"

Miguel flipped the rest of the triggers.

The entire building quaked as the remaining floors with rigged explosives detonated. The sound was tremendous, the reverberations flipping them both across the floor. Rubble and wreckage flew out from above and hit the streets, adding to the cacophonous bedlam outside. The walls surrounding them immediately ruptured, cracks ripping through the concrete and dry wall like lightning bolts. The glass atrium in the front lobby erupted, shards of twinkling glass cascading in all directions.

Screaming, Rocky tried to crawl on his hands and knees toward the front exit. Miguel rolled his way, blood smearing beneath him, and reached for Rocky's ankle. He dug his hand into the other man's open wound, burying his fingers as far in as they would go. Rocky squealed and fell flat to his stomach. Despite the pain in his gut, Miguel inched forward and then slowly pushed the letter opener into Rocky's side. Unable to move, Rocky continued to scream, beating the floor with his fists. When the blade would go no further, Miguel placed his palm onto the bottom of the hilt and pushed as hard as he could, bellowing into Rocky's face as the rest of the blade slid through his organs and disappeared into his body.

EVERYBODY WANTS TO RULE THE WORLD

Miguel finally collapsed on his back. His entire body had flushed numb. A ripple of cold whipped through his extremities, and soon those extremities no longer allowed movement. He could only turn his head and face the man who was once his best friend, his brother, as they both bled out.

"I…" Rocky huffed, his nose pressed into the linoleum floor. "I…don't…want to…die…Miggy…"

"Hey, Rock?" Miguel coughed out a laugh. "Bravo."

Rocky screamed hard.

As the upper half began to collapse and the rest of the building came roaring down to greet them, Miguel closed his tired eye and smiled, thinking of the little girl he had never met before and how her mother would be there to hold her in the morning as a new dawn rose to greet them.

"Bravo indeed."

RIVERS OF MERCY

WILE E. YOUNG

Owen had always been a stickler for the rules, I'd always thought the straps on life jackets were too tight. My dad used to pull me behind the boat on an inflatable tube. With a lifejacket felt like wearing a medieval suit of armor—cumbersome and uncomfortable.

We had stayed overnight at the Rompond Lodge, a timber and glass affair that sat on the edge of a mountain and overlooked the silver stream of the Trisonee River. Jordan had spent the night making periodic pilgrimages to the wine cellar, a lush in name and deed.

Her husband, Trevon, on the other hand, had spent the night regaling all of us with the stories of our past trips down the various rivers of the Ozarks. Owen had laughed, socialized with our friends, and generally ignored me through the evening, which lately had been the way I liked it.

WILE E. YOUNG

Through the night's frivolities, I'd just tried to grin and bear it for the sake of our friends. This trip had been a tradition for the past eight years, ostensibly started for me, according to Owen at least. Healing, catharsis, a chance for me to move on with my life. I could admit that the time spent in the white water numbed the pain when in the heat of things.

Owen kept saying that we should move on, but how do you move on after you lose a child? She'd been playing just outside, then she was gone. That had been a year of tears, and every year that followed brought more. I lost count of the sleepless nights, the ones where I had lain awake clutching a picture of my daughter and wondering.

My mind couldn't rest, and at one point it had me thinking about how easy it would be to step out of existence.

"Yo, Sophie! Are you just going to stand there all day? Let's get on the river," Owen shouted.

I'd zoned out, lost in the warmth of depression, but it didn't stop me from casting a withering glare at my husband. Owen didn't notice, having already reminded me that I was a perpetual thief of joy.

The outfitters had finished unloading, leaving them with a few complimentary trash bags, our paddles, and the three canoes. It was an overcast day, the clouds drifting low through the canyon, obscuring the cliffs.

I did have to admit that the Trisonee River *was* beautiful; cool green ivy grew on the rock walls that disappeared into the murky grey sky. The water was nice and cool, running in comforting blue and green currents and disappearing into the distant mist.

RIVERS OF MERCY

Amy would have loved this.

The thought of my missing daughter brought back the awful gnawing despair. I could picture her, fourteen years old now and full of life, a big pair of swimming goggles on her face and looking for crawdads.

I followed that fantasy until I was waist deep in the river, letting myself sink into my imagination, until I heard Owen hollering for me. I took a deep breath and headed back, reaching for my towel and the dry shorts I'd laid out.

"Have a nice swim?" Owen asked as he pulled a strap across our ice chest, making sure it fit snugly in the middle of the canoe next to our tent.

I didn't want to answer him, or more accurately, lie. Any mention of our daughter was sure to put Owen in a foul mood. It was half the reason our marriage was on more rocks than the ones in the river.

I had just climbed in and positioned myself in the front of the canoe when another came drifting by, this one a bright yellow and containing my friend, Liz. We'd known each other since the third grade and were basically inseparable, enough so that I had named Liz godmother.

It was unfortunate that Liz had married a complete tool. Ever since she'd met Steven Lloyd, she'd been under his heel. Liz always smiled and denied it, but I had seen her regress from a smart, if socially awkward, woman to a church mouse who glanced at her husband before she spoke.

Steven had a closely shaved black beard, worked out religiously, and had tacky tribal tattoos covering his arms that would one day be featured in the museum of human misery. And unfortunately for both Jordan and myself, our husbands couldn't get enough of him.

"We're hurrying! Sophie decided that she wanted a quick dip," Owen hollered.

Steven pounded the water with his paddle, sending a spray over Liz, who grimaced and forced a smile. Her eyes met mine and she gave a quick shake of her head, begging me not to say anything or make a scene.

If we're lucky, he'll drown today.

It was an ugly thought, but I had long stopped giving a shit when it came to Steven Lloyd.

"Are you ready, babe?" Owen called from the rear, paddle at the ready.

I flashed him a thumb's up and picked up the paddle. I felt the grinding of the canoe bottom against the gravel beach as Owen pushed off the shore. It didn't take long for the rolling current to catch us and begin the push down river.

Jordan and Trevon were waiting where the bend turned out of sight, anchored to a tree that had toppled into the river. Jordan lounged back with her feet up as she lay across their ice chest without a care in the world.

Trevon whooped and gave Steven a high-five as they floated past, the latter noticing the sunglasses that shielded Jordan's closed eyes. The two men locked eyes with each other wearing matching grins that were devoid of anything that resembled joy.

Steven dipped his paddle in the water, pushing it deep, then heaved as fast and hard as he could, sending a shower of water over Jordan who came to with a shrill gasp. Her curses fell on deaf ears as both men devolved into peals of laughter as she scrambled to find a blanket to warm herself against the chill morning.

I reached out with my paddle and gently guided our own vessel past Steven and Liz, she cast a long-suffering look that I refused to bite down on.

It was 28 miles to the takeout point, three days of socialization between all of us, and I hoped it would pass faster than I could blink.

❇️

The trip down the river was for the most part uneventful. The stones that rose from the river were smooth and cool to the touch, ivy grew across the canyon walls. Sometimes, we would pass a stream of water spiraling down the rocks, and Owen would steer directly into it. The water was cold, colder even than the river, and I gasped as Owen howled in excitement, Trevon and Steven joining the cry.

He smiled at me and I thought it was brilliant. He used to smile like that all the time, and I could return that joy. Since it'd happened, I'd learned how to fake happiness, or at least keep the constant pity at bay. I smiled back at him, but I didn't mean it.

We were going to get a divorce; I knew it in my gut. Marriages could survive the death of a child, if both partners were willing to work through the shared pain. But Owen had gotten past the pain, had decided to put away his grief and act like Amy had never existed. My spirit had been broken and I was just going through the motions until some random accident or neglect of myself finally put an end to me.

We stopped periodically throughout the day. Liz had brought along pre-packed sandwiches that she handed out as Jordan and I set up chairs on the bank.

Owen led the men in what started as river football, before devolving into an undeclared blood sport. They uttered battle cries, throwing each other into the water whenever one of them caught the neon green football they'd brought.

"It's like watching a bunch of Neanderthals," Liz mused as she took a bite.

Jordan sprayed another round of SPF, "I don't know about you ladies, but I'm tired of the yearly camping trips."

"I've always wanted to go to Cancun," Liz said, wiping her glasses down with a dry paper towel and holding them up to the light to make sure that she had successfully removed every inch of grime.

I kept quiet. Alternate vacation talk was all well and good, but at the end of the day our group was beholden to tradition, and that same tradition kept us anchored to the whims of whatever our husbands had set for us.

Liz blamed Steven. Trevon had once been studious and caring. That was what had attracted Jordan to him in the first place. She'd run the gamut of fuckboys that had given her a broken heart and plenty of discarded clothes left with her like trophies.

Now, just like Owen, he was slowly morphing into another self-proclaimed and obsessed "alpha-male." I thought it was all bullshit, because it was, but I could see the appeal for men. Silent submissive women? A confidence that bordered on delusion? Never having to second-guess or compromise? Who wouldn't want that?

Owen came splashing out of the shallows, turning to throw the football back to his cohorts. He shook like a dog, showering me with secondhand river water. He didn't bother going for his own chair, just sitting on the rocks, leaving a dark imprint on the dry stone.

"Have a good lunch?" he asked.

I nodded, trying to muster a smile. He looked hopeful before a quick flash of frustration once my frown and silence returned. I tried to distract him. "How much farther are we going today?"

Owen looked at the fading sun disappearing behind the cliffs that bordered the other side of the river. "Maybe another mile or two. Can't be out on the water too long; we don't want to tip over in the dark."

That was true. Jordan and Trevon had both gone in the drink when navigating a particularly tricky patch of rapids. We'd spent the better part of an hour fishing all of their valuables out of the river, and even then, we'd lost a backpack full of food that sunk straight to the bottom.

He slapped a hand on my exposed leg, smearing the sunscreen. "Speaking of that, we need to get going. I'm pretty sure that there is slow water ahead."

He whistled to the other men and hollered for them to get packing. Steven immediately sprinted through the river towards his canoe, screaming loudly enough that it sent a flock of birds winging from the trees.

Liz cast a withering glare at her husband, but made sure that his back was turned. She caught my eye and the disgust was wiped away like a dry erase board, replaced with a fake smile.

Jordan had ignored both of us, strutting towards her canoe with chair in hand, shoving it into Trevon's waiting arms.

It didn't take long to get back on the river. After the whitewater we'd been dealing with for most of the day, I was grateful for the slow current that barely seemed like it was moving. I was also grateful that Steven seemed to be running out of steam as the day wore on, but I still wanted to hit him as I saw Liz strain to keep them moving, and their canoe steadily fell behind us.

Owen whistled the entire time; I didn't recognize the tune. Besides the dip of our paddles and Owen's piping, the world was silent. I'd thought I was immune from the fears of the world since Amy, but the quiet sent a wave of chills racing up my arms. The sun had disappeared behind the cliffs, leaving the valley we were paddling through in a sea of purple and orange as evening arrived.

Owen leaned forward, rummaging through the pack until he pulled out a pair of binoculars. "We need to start looking for camp."

I didn't hesitate to throw a barb. "And you need binoculars for that?"

Owen's smile faltered for a minute, and I could tell that he was wrestling with the urge to fire back.

I knew that I shouldn't blame him for Amy. He'd been in his office, she'd been outside playing, just like we both had when we were kids. It had been the middle of the damn day even... But it was on his watch and she was gone.

I couldn't forgive that.

He didn't rise to the insult. Instead, he scanned for where we would stay for the night. I looked back, staring upriver and trying to pick out Liz and Steven in the swiftly gathering gloom. It was hard to see, and their dark red canoe could have easily camouflaged itself against one of the rocks, but after a few seconds of searching, I decided they must've fallen far enough behind that they were past the bend.

Owen whistled sharply to Trevon. "About a quarter mile up! There's a good beach by a tidal island. Let's stop there for the night!"

Trevon gave a thumbs up and both men began to paddle harder. I saw Jordan turn in the seat, carefully adjusting so she wouldn't tip the canoe here at the end of the day. She cupped her hands and yelled, "Where's Liz?"

I shrugged. "I don't know! She was the only one paddling!"

I was about to suggest turning around when Owen spoke up. "You shouldn't worry about them."

That was news to me. "Yeah? It's getting dark, Owen. What if they get lost?"

He kept smiling that same infuriating grin and waggled his eyebrows. "Steven told me that he was interested in a little private time outdoors. Said he's always wanted to try it."

I didn't know how to respond to that with anything other than pity. I could just imagine Liz on their cheap blowup mattress surrounded by the fading humidity and biting mosquitoes.

WILE E. YOUNG

⁂

The sunlight was almost gone, and our friends had still not arrived. The night was all around us; I couldn't see more than thirty yards upriver and that was only thanks to the fire that Trevon had built. Distantly, I saw flashes of lighting, and then a rolling peel of thunder came rumbling through the canyon.

Owen appeared, chewing on a piece of jerky. "Don't worry, we're not getting rained on. That storm has to be thirty miles away, and it's not moving toward us."

"I don't care about that. Are you not worried that Steven and Liz haven't shown up?"

I watched him chew, not even bothering to close his mouth. He shrugged. "They're having a good time. It's slow water, they'll be fine."

I sighed and stalked back to my chair, practically throwing myself into it and ignoring Jordan and Trevon who were doing their best to pretend like they were not there.

I kept my eyes on the fire, watching it dance. I heard the rocks shift as Jordan moved closer. Owen returned and was excitedly talking to Trevon about some new development in their fantasy league that we barely paid attention to.

"I've got a bad feeling," I whispered and looked over at her.

She had traded her bikini for a baggy hoodie and sweats, but she wrapped her arms around herself like the cold was closing in. "Yeah, me too."

Jordan watched our husbands, busy wrangling the griddle over the fire so we could start dinner, "It's just a feeling. I can't put my finger on it, but I just don't feel comfortable out here." She looked around at the encroaching darkness. "Just feels like we're being watched."

I reached down and poked the fire with a loose twig, stirring up the flame and sending a shower of sparks billowing into the night. "I know what you mean, and where are Steven and Liz?"

Jordan leaned over eyeing the men. "And why don't they care? That asshole is one of their best friends and they're acting like he just went down the street for a few beers."

I was about to suggest that maybe we should hike upriver a bit and see if we could find where Steven and Liz might have stopped when a loud snap echoed behind us.

I shot out of my chair as Jordan twisted around, looking towards the tree line. Owen glanced up from his ministrations. "You two are jumpy. It's probably just a squirrel."

"What if it's a bear?" Jordan hissed causing Trevon to slowly stand, holding the pair of tongs he'd been using like a sword.

Owen placed a skillet full of vegetables over the flame, not even bothering to act concerned. "A bear isn't going to wander into a camp with four people in it. They're scared of fire."

Pretty much everything was scared of fire, but I didn't want to test that theory if there was an actual bear in the woods. I stood, facing the trees; I didn't want to have my back exposed if six hundred pounds of angry predator came charging from the dark.

Owen crept forward, a small pocketknife clutched tight. It was like the white noise of the world suddenly rushed in around me. I could hear the pounding rapids at the bank, the crickets chirping their song to the evening, the crackling fire that spit sparks…

I saw movement, barely a silhouette against the trees, and then the fire cast its warm glow on pale dirty skin. Feet that were cut and stained with old, dried blood walked across sharp rocks without care, and I saw the firelight dance off dull and hollow eyes.

The naked girl walked towards the fire without care that we were there. She couldn't have been more than eleven, and I saw my husband's wide eyes watch her all the way to the flame.

"Christ…" Trevon whispered, and Jordan moved forward, spare blanket in hand, draping around the girl's shoulders to conceal her. I crouched next to her, reaching for her hand.

"Sweetie… sweetie? What happened?" I asked.

The girl kept staring at the flames, rocking back and forth on her feet, her mouth clenched in a firm line. Jordan grabbed her own chair, and we slowly guided the girl until she was sitting.

Owen and Trevon were whispering to each other, glancing at the girl between their hushed words.

"What is it?" I asked.

Owen looked to the woods and then back at me. "There might be more. Or someone could need help."

I cupped my hands and shouted, "HELLO, IS THERE ANY—"

Jordan shouted behind me, and I suddenly felt a sharp grip on my arm. The girl looked up at me, eyes streaming tears, furiously shaking her head. Her eyes were rooted on the woods, and I thought it best I didn't look.

There could be someone there. Watching.

The thought came unheeded, but I reassured the girl, guiding her back to the chair. I looked to Owen, "We need to call the police."

He chuckled like I had just asked if we could walk to Venus. "How? We're in the middle of nowhere. There's no signal."

I kept my voice down. The girl wasn't looking towards us, but I didn't want to scare her by yelling. "Then let's get in a boat and go! I'm not staying here for the night."

"There's no way we're making it down the river at night. It's too risky," Trevon said, pointing the tongs up the hill. "That's probably what happened to her; parents overturned or something."

I couldn't believe what I was hearing, like every bit of reason these two had between them had dried off with their swim trunks. "That's bullshit, Trevon. She came from the fucking woods. And even if she didn't then you're saying we shouldn't go find help for her parents?"

He looked to Owen for help, and I met my husband's eyes, letting the unsaid words pass between us. *This is your chance. OUR chance. We couldn't help Amy, but we can save this girl.*

If you've never known someone, really know them, then it's hard to explain reaching out with your heart and hoping they do the same. I could feel his frustration, his desire and his wants dueling for what was right.

And I felt the black curtain of numbness wrap itself across my shoulders when he shook his head. "Trevon's right. Navigating in the night would be suicide."

The matchwood of our marriage broke there, and the bitter resolve of "irreconcilable differences" settled in. I didn't say another word as I rejoined Jordan and the girl.

Trevon returned to his position by the fire, smiling at the girl as he stirred the small skillet of vegetables. "Let's get you something to eat."

Jordan gave her husband a warm smile, but quickly turned back to the girl. "Can you tell us your name?"

The girl didn't respond, and anything that we tried to ask her was met with a similar silence. After twenty minutes or so, Trevon passed a plate of food to us, and I cut the steak he'd grilled in half.

"Are you hungry?" I asked.

The girl reached with trembling hands for the food. I put my half of the meat on my own plate, nibbling at it, my appetite gone. She devoured her food with her hands, foregoing the fork I'd handed her. But the steak knife was kept in easy reach.

Jordan and I locked eyes, a similar thought passing between us, one that didn't need to be said. If you were a woman in this world, or a girl, you knew what was potentially waiting in the dark corners of alleyways, churches, and the marriage bed.

Trevon ate quietly, only giving us an awkward glance from time to time. Owen paced at the edge of the river, occasionally stopping to crouch and wash his hands in the water. He never looked at us, didn't care that there was a naked girl protected from the elements by a Razorbacks blanket in his chair. I wondered if he was thinking of us… or Amy…

It would have given me hope to think he cared that much.

Jordan and I both decided that it was best for us to bunk in the same tent, the girl with us. If what we thought had happened was true, I doubted she wanted to be alone with two strange men.

I unzipped the tent in one swift pull, climbing in and rifling through my pack until I found my spare sleep shirt. Jordan guided the girl onto the air mattress, a thick number that could survive Owen's tossing and turning on the rocks.

Jordan closed the tent while I gently reached to remove the blanket from the girl. I saw her hands tighten, and I tried to smile as gently as I could, offering her the shirt. "It's ok. This won't fit, but it's super long and comfortable."

Her eyes jumped between Jordan and I like she was watching two dangerous animals, but she eventually took it. Enveloped in the shirt, she curled up on the air mattress, arms wrapped around her legs like a babe from the womb.

Jordan leaned to me, whispering gently, "Are you thinking what I'm thinking?"

I looked at the girl's bare feet. Her cuts were old, but there were crisscrossed scars across her soles, old wounds that had been deep.

"Yeah, I think I am."

There was the sound of crunching rocks, footsteps, and a black shadow appeared over the tarp.

"Run." It was a small sound, but it echoed through the tent like a gunshot: the girl had spoken. She was tense, her hands clenching the mattress tight, and she whispered again, "Run."

I glanced at the shadow, then back to the girl, and then around the tent wondering if my husband had another knife in here or in the canoe.

"Everything ok in there?" Trevon asked.

I breathed a sigh of relief and watched Jordan chuckle a bit. "Yeah, babe, we're all good. I think we're going to see if we can get her to sleep."

He didn't answer for a moment, but I had the distinct sense that he was listening. "Ok, good, glad she's doing ok. I think Owen and I are going to try for some late-night fishing."

I took over for my friend, walking with my knees across the air mattress until I was near the tent opening. "Alright, you guys have fun!" It was chipper, at ease, and a lie. I couldn't understand how these men could still act like we were on a normal camping trip, like a naked pre-teen hadn't come walking out of the woods.

Trevon retreated, his footsteps crunching in the loose gravel. I reached for the zipper and unwound just enough so that I could see. Owen was just an undefined figure at the edge of the river, rod and reel in hand, highlighted by the flicker of flame against his yellow shirt.

He never came to wish us good night or check on me.

✳

There was a sharp crack of thunder and I came to from sleep's grip. The wind was whipping hard, and the sharp patter of raindrops against the fabric sounded like an avalanche of rocks.

It's 30 miles away, it's not going to storm on us.

That had been Owen's assertion and he'd been wrong, but that wasn't something new. As long as we'd been married, he'd had a self-assurance that bordered on delusion. Even when presented with proof, he'd try to twist it so that he didn't come off looking completely wrong. But it seemed to keep happening.

I glanced at my bedmates. Jordan was wrapped up tight in her sleeping bag, but she'd given up her pillow for the girl, motionless under a blanket between me and her. Both were fast asleep.

Lightning flashed, temporarily turning the night white. My heart began to beat faster when I thought about Liz, wondering if they had ever made it to us. I was quiet, barely pulling at the zipper.

I craned my head out, catching drops on my face as the wind shifted. Our campsite was a mess, our chairs blown over and drenched through, but the fire was still a dim glowing orange, wisps of smoke visible when the lightning flashed. The other tent was wide open, the entrance tarp flapping in the storm.

The river was a lot closer than when we had gone to bed. I could see the current churning in the brief flashes of white light from the sky's fire. Logs and debris were hurtling past smashing together in the murk and turning the river into a quagmire. It was only ten or so yards away and rising.

I turned around and shook Jordan as hard as I could. "Get your ass up, we've gotta get out of here now!"

The girl shot up, looking like a pale ghost in the oversized shirt. Jordan floundered for a moment, fighting her sleep and trying to understand what was happening. She pressed down onto the tarp and immediately jerked it out. I saw that it was dripping wet from where the water was already beginning to work its way under the tent.

I bundled the girl up in my arms, feeling her legs wrap around me as I shouted, "Come on!"

There was no time to change or shield ourselves against the elements; the water was already at the entrance. I splashed out, feeling the torrent of rain drench my clothes, sending a chill through my skin.

Thunder roared, and there was hiss of steam as the river reached the nearly dead campfire. "We need to get to high ground!"

Jordan could barely hear me over the din, but she gave a thumbs up and we both began to flee, feeling the sharp stones press into my feet with every step. Our trek was more of a hobble.

Jordan wasn't faring better. I could hear her pained grunting and the shifting stones, then I heard her cry as the rocks moved and she went to her knees, scraping them raw. I went to help her, cradling the girl with one hand as I helped Jordan to her feet, she bit her lip when her legs flexed, trying to ignore the pain.

Our tents were halfway under, the pegs anchored tight the only reason they weren't floating halfway down the bend. We made it to the tree line when they finally came loose, tumbling end over end until they were dragged under.

The trees provided a little cover, but the dark swallowed us as we plunged into the canopy. Water poured off the surrounding tree limbs like miniature waterfalls. My hair clung to my face like a veil and I had trouble discerning the path ahead. But behind me I could hear the rush of the river as it swept up the banks.

I didn't have a plan, any idea of where to go, just up, always up. Far enough that the water couldn't reach us. The girl's hands tightened around my neck as I struggled to part leaves and tree limbs that were only illuminated when the lightning crashed.

"Where are we going!?" Jordan hollered, her voice sounding like some phantom carried on the winds. I didn't have any idea where we were going, the woods surrounding us in a grotesque wooden maze.

My heart beat fast, and the Ozark mountain chill bit deep into my bones. The rain was cold, and the air was its companion. Thoughts of pneumonia and freezing to death in these conditions began to run through my mind. Then came another sound, small against the roaring storm. I heard my name being shouted.

"SOPHIE!!!" It was Owen, and despite our troubles, I was glad to hear his voice.

"OVER HERE!" I hollered, cupping my hand to my mouth so my voice would carry. I couldn't tell which direction my husband's voice was coming from, but I plunged into the undergrowth hoping that I had guessed right. His voice came again, louder, closer, and I saw a bobbing white light beyond the next copse of trees.

Owen emerged out of the gloom, and for a moment, the old feelings that had seen us fall in love reignited. I didn't care about the girl clutched in my arms, or the fact that it was raining, or that he had even disappeared in the first place. He was here now, and that was all that mattered.

One hand holding onto the girl, I embraced my husband, feeling the warmth of his chest, and for a moment, imagined that the girl in my arm was Amy. When I pulled back, I realized that we weren't alone; Trevon was close by. He was the one clutching the lantern, but there were others with them. They were all dressed in outdoor wear, prepared for the weather better than us.

Trevon moved to embrace his own wife, taking off the soaked jacket and wrapping it around her shoulders like it had even the slightest chance in hell of warming her up. The three strangers in the ponchos watched, their flashlight glows glinting off their eyes. In the downpouring night, I thought they looked like shards of black ice. Those eyes looked over Jordan and I, impassive, uncaring... until they saw the girl held in my arms. They didn't stop looking at her and I felt her hands tighten around my neck when she saw them.

The one in the middle walked forward, a hand outstretched. "Oh, thank god you found her!"

The girl clawed at my neck and I heard a tiny voice in my ear whisper, "Layla, that's my name."

It was a tiny whisper, like the coo of a bird. I almost thought that I had imagined it, but I still took a step away from the man and looked at my husband. "Owen, who are these guys?"

RIVERS OF MERCY

Owen placed a comforting hand on my shoulder, hollering over the downpour. "This is Leon and his friends. They're taking their kids camping. His daughter wandered off and we found her!"

Leon nodded, shaking his head to clear his vision. "And we really don't have time to meet properly. Look!" He pointed and I saw that the river had found us.

Trees fell behind us in crashes of earth that were swept away just as fast. Owen pointed up the hill. "They have a car! They can get us out of here, we've just got to get to high ground."

The strangers leading the way, Owen grabbed my hand and pulled me forward while Trevon ushered Jordan behind us. The whole valley behind us had to be underwater, I assumed we were on a trail that was heading up the mountain.

I tried and failed to get my husband's attention; he had the convenience store machete he'd bought two days beforehand and was slashing at the leaves in clumsy strokes. The rain may have been letting up, but no one called for us to stop. The trees began to thin, and then we were at a metal guardrail.

Jordan's pants mixed with mine. We must've hiked a half mile straight up the mountain, and I could tell that both of us were beginning to feel it. There were two vehicles waiting, a van and a four-door truck, both idling.

Rain evaporated off the hood, and I saw Leon gesture to the van, his two companions veering off towards it. He turned and smiled, pointing to the van. "Sarah and I are riding in the truck. You guys can ride with Alan in the van."

WILE E. YOUNG

One of the other men in the rain ponchos waved as he flashed a key ring. Leon didn't waste time, approaching me and reaching for the girl, who began to sob and claw at my neck.

Call it maternal instinct, or the sense that I was prey in the midst of predators, or that these men were scaring a little girl.

Or maybe it was just the right thing to do.

I flinched away from him, making sure he couldn't touch her. "What did you say her name was?"

For a second, I saw a flash of hate flicker through his gaze. "What did you say?"

I stepped back, staring the man down. "What's… her… name?"

The hairs on the back of my neck were standing up and this man, Leon, stared me down before finally shaking his head. A laugh escaped his lips that had absolutely no joy in it. "Does it fucking matter?"

His fist found my face and then I was on the ground. The pain began as the rain fell directly into my abused eye. I gripped the girl, holding tight, and felt her slip from my arms. I heard sobbing and then two swift slaps. The sobbing stopped.

Jordan was screaming, but it sounded far away. I didn't think she could scream like that. Then she was begging, another smacking sound, and it was just quiet sobbing.

Strong hands lifted me up and I saw my husband from my good eye. His eyes were dead, lifeless, like he was looking at something inanimate, something that didn't stoke fire in him. Something he didn't care about.

"Owen…" I whispered, the pain garbling my words.

The rain splattered into my open eye, causing me to blink, and every single time the world around me changed. First there was the asphalt and my husband, then there were arms supporting me, and the tableau of the black night sky.

Finally, I was inside the van, and I heard screaming.

My hands were wrenched behind me, and I felt the rough edges of a zip tie wind tight. The scene swirled and came into focus, and I saw Jordan thrash on the seat as Trevon used a knife to carve furrows in the soles of her feet.

I wanted to scream, but my voice only came out in a small hoarse cough. "Help."

Owen looked at me, shaking his head. "Just stop."

The door opened and I heard a peal of thunder, and the driver took his place, dripping water. His voice was flavored with an accent that I couldn't place. "They secure?"

Owen nodded and the man started the engine. The scent of the van assaulted my senses, heavy and coppery, and I realized that the floor and seats were stained brown. Jordan's bleeding feet gave me a good idea where those stains had come from.

Trevon grasped his wife's feet tight, looking at her unblemished heel, and then began to work on that too. I began to scream, thrashing in my seat. "LEAVE HER ALONE!"

Her husband didn't even glance at me before rubbing the knife in her hair, lathering it with her own blood. I strained against the tie, rubbing my wrists raw. "FUCKER, YOU FUC—"

It was Owen's hand that lashed out this time, his palm leaving a stinging welt across my face and drawing fresh blood as my lip drug across my teeth. A finger lifted my chin, turning it back. "Sophie... shut the fuck up." He sighed, a weary smile gracing his features. "I've waited a long time to tell you that."

I wanted a gun, a knife, anything that I could use to hurt him. There was no processing, no working through what was happening, and there had been so little love between us that I didn't mourn its demise. My fear and worry for my friend was all I had left, that and the confusion. Why were they doing this to us?

Owen watched Trevon do his work while he addressed me. "I thought things might get better after Amy. Sure you'd grieve, but you'd move on. Thing is, you never fucking moved on." He ran a finger across the window. "You just kept looking, waiting, hoping she'd come back. And you ignored me, of course. Like you always have."

The truck bounced as he ran that cold finger across my right foot. I jerked away and spit at him, but the blob of saliva fell short. He shook his head and I saw something that resembled guilt in his eyes. "I didn't want a kid, said it over and over. But you didn't listen. So when you saddled me with that squalling thing, I got to thinking..."

"Can we blind them?" Trevon asked, waving the box cutter over his wife's eyes as Jordan clenched them tight, fresh tears squeezing between her lashes.

RIVERS OF MERCY

The driver, Leon had called him Alan, shook his head. "No, buyers like pretty eyes… pretty feet too."

Trevon paled a little, but finally just settled into his seat, his hand roving across his wife's body, smiling like he was exploring familiar territory.

"It took a few years, but I found some people willing to make money off a child. Didn't even have to pay them, they paid me." Owen's smile was wistful and I strained at the plastic around my wrists, feeling the tears in my eyes as my vision narrowed and each word stabbed like a knife.

"Remember that trip to Playa Del Carmen we went on after they took her? The first vacation afterwards? The one our therapist said would be good for us? Amy paid for it."

I screamed, throwing myself at the disgusting thing that had taken my child, gnashing with my teeth for his throat, praying that before they did whatever it was they had planned for me, that I could just taste this man's blood.

His hands shoved me back into the center console, hard, and he leaned in, his lips brushing my ears. "Afterwards, I waited for you to get better, but that didn't happen. And when I brought it up to the guys, it turned out they were having their own marital troubles."

My stomach churned as I felt his tongue wind its way down my earlobe, and I wrenched my head to bite, but he pulled away faster than a snake. "Turns out Leon and his crew will take more than just kids."

Trevon passed the box cutter to Owen. I watched it like it was a wasp, flexing my feet, already feeling the phantom bite of the blade.

He waved the blade in front of my eyes. "That way you can't run."

I closed my eyes and I heard a cracking noise and the world went end over end. The windows shattered and I hit the seat, then the wall. The men were screaming, but it faded to nothing.

Rain pattered against my face and, for a moment in the sweet void of insensate darkness, there was no pain, and my daughter was waiting for me. I heard weak groaning and the steady rain against the crushed metal. I opened my eyes to blackness, the only illumination coming from the brief flashes of lightning. I tried to move, feeling aches run through my entire body.

Another lightning strike revealed that the van was half-full of watery runoff that was flowing through the windows, slowly moving the crushed van like we were floating on some gentle stream.

Landslide, the word flickered through my brain as I realized that the road had given way and sent us tumbling down the slope. My hands brushed against something sharp. I couldn't tell if it was the box cutter or a broken shard of glass, and I didn't care. My grip on the shard slipped more than once, adding my blood to the mix of dirt and water rushing through the wreck. The zip tie finally snapped as lightning showed me the distended and blank face of the driver.

RIVERS OF MERCY

The steering console had been shoved through his chest cavity, pinning him against the seat. His mouth was hanging open, blood dripping from his teeth, and his eyes were pinned on me.

A deep moan echoed in the dark. I turned, rolling through the muck to find a handhold. Every new movement sent dull aches through me, and I hissed into the black. "Jordan!"

I heard a soft cry, and I waved my hands around, feeling something warm run down my wrists where I'd nicked them. The van was upside down and I moved across the crumpled metal as carefully as I could.

I stepped on something soft.

Dropping to my knees, I felt wet flesh, searching for hair or breasts, and recoiling when I felt the firm chest. I didn't know if it was Owen or Trevon, and I didn't care. I crawled over him, my hands embedding themselves on cut glass and wet muck.

It seemed like an eternity in the dark, but I finally felt long wet strands of hair and felt my friend's soft features under my searching touch. "Jordan... JORDAN!"

She stirred. I heard her mumble my name, but my relief was short lived as I heard the muttered cursing as the remaining men began to wake. The rear window had also shattered, but it was the only one that didn't have a steady stream of mud pouring through it.

The glass on my skin and ruined pajamas was unforgiving, but there was something in me now that didn't care about the fresh lacerations, something ugly, something that wanted to hurt. Mourning turned to murder.

WILE E. YOUNG

I felt the fresh shock of the cold rain, but the cold in me was deeper than the thunderstorm coating the Ozarks. I turned around and reached back inside for Jordan, feeling her arms and pulling as hard as I could. She was dead weight until I dragged her over the glass. Her eyes popped open and she began to scream, a howl that was cut off by the thunder. I pressed a finger to her lips, hoping I could quiet her, but it was too late.

There was a sudden tug and a myriad of profanity, and Jordan squealed as she was dragged back over the glass, my fingers desperately digging into her wet skin. It sounded like both of them had come out of it. Jordan's nails dug into my arms as I screamed, desperately trying to hang on. Her arms and head were the only things still outside of the car.

I could see them, dark figures with contorted and rage filled faces, their eyes reflected in the quick flares of lightning. Jordan looked up at me with wide eyes, dead eyes, and she said, "Go, Sophie. Run."

Then she let go of me and her wet arms slid out of my grasp and into the darkness of the wrecked van. She was screaming when I turned my back, listening to the wet impact of fists on flesh, and before I let the water take me, I saw Owen crawling through the window, bleeding and screaming at me like a wounded animal.

I slid on the mud under me, hitting the ground and falling with the water into the dark. It carried me down, runoff and rooted limbs scratching and tearing at me.

My stomach dropped when the ground suddenly disappeared, and I plunged through empty air. A ten-foot drop and a soft landing on dirt didn't save the wind from being knocked out of me.

The night hid me, but I heard the faint shouts, my husband looking for me. The cold and ugly thing that had awoken in me forced me up onto my knees, breathing heavy and swallowing the rain drops coming down between the trees above me. I took a staggering step, my bare feet cushioned by the mud, and fumbled my way through the dark.

I didn't have an idea of what to do, where to go, just away. I wondered if I would freeze to death huddled in a clutch of bushes. There would be no regret in it, other than the fact that Owen was still alive.

He sold our daughter.

That was the thought that drove me now, letting the anger feed me as I fed it in turn, and suddenly I was unaware of the cold around me. Above the constant rain, I heard a churning sound and thought that I must finally have made it to the surging river, but faintly there was something else…

I realized it was a car horn.

I followed the noise, letting the storm mask the sound of crushed leaves and snapped branches. Eventually, I saw faint traces of light. It grew brighter until I made out the black truck that Leon had taken the little girl into.

It was on its side, crushed against a tree, a victim of the same landslide. Leon was nowhere to be seen, but I could hear groaning sobs coming from the man hanging halfway out of the broken windshield. He saw me move from the bushes and began to beg, until he saw who it was that had found him.

"Oh Christ..."

I ignored him. The truck was badly damaged; the seats had been moved and the chassis crushed down, if there was anyone in the backseat, they wouldn't have been able to get out. But I had hope and was rewarded when I saw two tiny eyes staring back at me.

"Hang on!" I shouted, and watched the eyes disappear. I felt between the injured man's seat, ignoring his whimpers, and finally wrapped my hand around the seat adjuster. I pulled upward, feeling the resistance as the metal ground together, and then the satisfying CLICK when it slotted into place.

I pulled forward and felt a cold joy in my heart when the man screamed. I heard the cracking when his already tormented chest was dragged across the shattered glass, his trapped spine mangled further. I didn't care if he couldn't walk again.

The girl appeared in the gap, hands grasping the torn seatbacks and pulling herself into my waiting arms. I wrapped her up tight "I've got you, Amy, I've got you."

I felt her hands grasp my neck, and I heard a small voice say that something wasn't right, but I ignored it. She was with me again and that was all that mattered.

The man groaned again, gasping in a way that made me think his lungs were injured. I sat Amy on the ground, lowering myself until I was eye-level with her. "I have to take care of this bad man. Stay right here."

Amy nodded and I turned back, wiping the rain from my eyes as I worked my way around the wrecked truck until I was face-to-face with the nearly-dead man.

He tried to raise his head, but I grasped his hair and shoved it down, small chunks of glass working their way into his cheek.

"You took my daughter!" I growled, baring my teeth, enjoying his crying when I twisted his head deeper into the glass, hoping they would worm their way through. Maybe he would swallow them.

He tried to deny it. "I didn't… I didn't! I don't even know your daughter."

I pointed at Amy watching with big eyes. "That's her right there! She found me again."

My thumb pressed into the base of his neck where a dark and ugly bruise was slowly spreading. He screamed louder than the thunder that cracked in the distance. It felt like hard marbles rolling under his skin, and the more I separated them, the less he screamed.

He went slack, sliding down on the glass, but his eyes were wide with fresh tears. "I can't feel it. Christ, I can't feel it."

The man's neck jerked. He closed his eyes to avoid the rain and the glass halfway through his mouth. "Leon… you have to find… He'll, hel—"

I heard the patter of feet and then a tree limb, sodden with enough water that it was nearly black, plunged through the man's left eye. Amy twisted, drilling the stick deeper into his skull. The orb burst, spilling clear fluid and blood across the hood. His head jerked and his screaming reached a high-pitch keening as the rough bark made turn after turn deeper into his skull, then it died like a helium balloon...

His head thudded against the metal hood and his remaining eye watched us sightlessly. Amy collapsed in silent sobs that wracked her body and I reached for her, slowly picking her up in my arms and carrying her away from the truck.

"Shhhh, it's ok. You did what you had to, but mom has you."

She kept crying, and feeling her in my arms, I began to join her, sobs of sorrow mixing with my own tentative joy. My daughter was returned to me.

And that was all that mattered.

I didn't believe that there was anywhere free from the rain. The storm was beginning to pass, but everything seemed to be coated in the thick running drops. We would freeze soon in these elements. The chill had gone past my nerves and seemed to be biting into my aching bones.

My eyes had long since adjusted to the dark, but that barely helped in the search for shelter. The adrenaline was beginning to wear off and my arms ached from the strain of carrying my daughter, each step feeling like an Olympic feat.

There was nothing but the wet black. I walked parallel to the river and I could hear it rushing, along with the sounds of logs smashing into rocks and riverbed.

Amy was shivering against me; I could feel it even through the numbness of my skin, the comfortable warmth that I knew was just an illusion of the false cold that was slowly nipping away at my life. I wanted to lie down.

I was reminded of my times in college, staggering home after a heavy night, and suddenly the trees were no longer part of the forest, but windows and open doors of apartments. They looked safe… and warm.

There was no rain. I could feel dampness on the tile floors my mind had created, but the rain was behind me. The light faded and the imagined haven went with it, replaced by the dull wetness of a hollowed-out tree.

The bark was moist, and the rain didn't stop, but it didn't fall on us and I couldn't have been more grateful for it. I sank against the wood, registering the roughness against my skin.

I pulled Amy close and whispered to her, "It's ok, Amy. We'll get through this, we'll get home."

She looked up at me, eyes like marbles in the dark. Her mouth moved and I heard her voice, hoarse and unfamiliar, like she had forgotten how to use it. "That— That's not—"

I pressed a finger to her lip, "Yes, it is."

She quieted down and snuggled closer, and I felt the warmth between us.

Morning came with fresh bird song and the dim gray light of day. I opened my eyes slowly, blinking, looking at the damp brown leaves under me and the girl curled up in my arms.

I wiped my nose, feeling the thick clear drops of snot on the back of my hand. There was a fresh wave of chill bumps, and I clutched at the ground, feeling the wet earth squeeze between my fingers and the movement of worms.

There was no way to be sure where we were, but the animal instinct in me couldn't be ignored. Owen wouldn't stop looking for us, not now, not if there was the slightest chance we could make it back and bring his fucking life crashing down.

I gently woke Amy, feeling her fingers tighten around me as she looked around. Then she saw my face and the fear retreated. Her arms left my waist, wrapping around her stomach. The gurgle followed soon after, my own hunger calling in response. And I felt the worms.

I cupped my daughter's cheek and she stared at me, unsure, and I leaned in, hoping she could see the deep well of love that I was drawing from. "This will be hard, but we have to eat. You're not alone, I'm here."

She saw the wriggling things in my hand and didn't hesitate to reach for them, plucking a worm from the black soil and chewing. I saw the black guts spill over her teeth, a trail of mucus coating her lips.

I cupped her chin. "I'm proud of you."

She swallowed and bit her lip, trying to find the words that she wanted to say and failing. She wanted to know that I was proud of her, that I knew she was brave...

"You're a tough girl, you've had to be for nine years, and I'm sorry I wasn't there for you. But we're going to get out of here... and we're going to be happy."

The words poured out of me like a dam that had finally given way to building pressure. I meant every word, and it was all the things that I had always wanted to say to Amy.

She didn't smile back at me, didn't return my embrace. Her eyes had reverted to the blank emotionless stare she'd wandered back into my life with. Silently, we chewed our worms and listened to the birds sing their welcome to the gray day.

I wasn't sure of the time when we finally left the tree, and I was just as lost as I had been in the dark. The woods stretched away to our left, the little openings they gave us swallowed by more deep green. To my right, I heard the river.

It hadn't quieted from last night, and through gaps in the trees, I could see frothing white at the bottom of the slope. We would be exposed if we went down to the beach. If Owen and the others were watching for us, they would be on the river. Of course, they'd be on the road too, combing the woods…

There really wasn't much of a choice. At least on the water someone might float by who could help, or we would find a takeout site with good company.

Grabbing my daughter's hand, I nodded towards the river, putting on the bravest smile that I could. "Come on."

We took our time, trying to find solid footing as we made our way down. I helped Amy as best I could, taking her hand in mine as she shimmied down an embankment. I thought about Jordan and Liz and wondered if they were still alive. It seemed likely, men like this weren't usually in the habit of murdering product…

It seemed obvious now that Liz had probably vanished into one of the unmarked vehicles Leon had brought us to. I wondered if she was still there, trapped by a landslide and waiting to be rescued by the scum that had taken everything from me.

And Jordan, I didn't think I was ever going to forget the sounds she'd made.

I think that my pain protected me, the numbness that I had lived with for longer than I cared to think kept me shielded from the loss of my friends. Inside I had been dead and it was easy to throw the despair into the ever-gnawing pit at the bottom of my soul. It was well fed, but it could not eat the newfound spark that blazed in me, it could numb the pain, but it could not devour the fury.

There was no more shore, no graveled beaches to set up a tent. The water was a churning brown that rushed past, large bits of debris rolling over in the fierce current. A few trees jutted out from the water, the leaves on the branches clumped together in tight clusters. I saw flashes of color in the water, bits of shredded tents. I scanned the shore as far as I could see, looking for a boat or canoe that maybe come unmoored, something that we could use.

There was a groan and I saw a tree slowly disappear into the depths as great girders of gray steel suddenly poked themselves free of the current. I could see rebar and concrete and realized that I was looking at a bridge that had been swept away by the flood. I saw the metal ripple as it pressed into the riverbed, crumpling and disappearing and crushing the drowned trees under its artificial corpse. Then it went under and vanished back into the depths, replaced with the tranquil rushing water.

We went downriver, and I kept looking for a boat. The water lapped softly at our feet, and I picked Amy up to avoid the rocks. There were no people, none that we saw, but still we kept silent; the woods could have ears listening for us.

In the silence, other sounds may as well have been gunshots, so when I heard a steady and distinctive *thump*, we narrowed in on it. The canoe was nestled in some rocks. The craft was dark green, which was good; it wouldn't attract as much attention on the water.

I edged closer to it, but felt Amy pull back, rooted to the rocks where we were standing. Her mouth moved, and that small voice managed to whisper, "They'll see." Her eyes traveled across the river, to the peaks of green that disappeared into the low hanging clouds, and I wondered if she could see something I couldn't, if there was some animal instinct that whispered they could see us.

And in that moment, there was a faint noise. A long, distant horn that echoed around us and was gone. My daughter's hand, already tight, squeezed a little tighter.

I squeezed back, donning a reassuring smile. "Don't worry. Whatever it is, it can't hurt us."

Her wide eyes looked everywhere but me, and I reached out to grab her cheeks. Clasping her head in my hands, I tried to let her know that she was safe, that this was the best thing for us. "I know you're scared, but this will take us home faster. We can get help."

The wild eyes settled and she came with me. I picked her up and sat her in the front of the canoe. There was no paddle in the pools around us, and I decided that the current would have to be our guide.

145

WILE E. YOUNG

The water dropped off quickly away from the rocks, one swift dip was all it took to realize that. I scrambled in from the last rock, sitting down and feeling the strength of the water as we followed the current.

I never noticed the body we were dragging until Amy did. She turned around, looking at me with newfound curiosity, a daughter that hadn't seen her mother in years... but instead she gasped, scrambling to hide herself in the boat's hollow prow.

I immediately turned and stifled my gasp at the dead man floating behind us. His body was bloated, probably resting in the roiling water all night. A bright white rope was curled around him. It looked like he had tried to pull the canoe out of the water when the flooding started.

I thought about hauling him in, one tug of the rope was all it took to disabuse me of the notion, and I was afraid to look at the dead man's face. Slowly, I turned back around, careful not to rock the canoe and send us into the water with the corpse. I slipped my hands into the river, "Don't look at him. Sit back down and just look at the trees and the water."

It was empty reassurance, but it was all I had. A glance back at the dead man confirmed that he wasn't going to shake loose. He'd follow us like a fish too hurt to swim, hooked to us in a paltry funeral procession.

My reflection stared back at me from the dark water and I didn't recognize the dirty and dripping thing with empty eyes staring back at me. For all I knew, this was my soul, truly reflected and bared, released into the world, and it wondered how many other dead things were swimming beneath the keel of our canoe.

RIVERS OF MERCY

An hour passed, two, and at the top of each one, that long horn sounded like some clock counting down on the world. We looked upriver, but there was nothing there that we could see. I didn't know what it was, but it seemed to be coming faster now, shorter, and I tried to think about what kind of sound could be heard through the entire river valley.

It consumed me enough that I almost didn't hear the voices. The shore was mostly trees, but it looked like we were coming up on small outcroppings of rock that might have been cliffs just yesterday. There were flashes of brown logs and the scarce sunlight piercing through the overcast sky reflected off glass, I heard the voices more clearly.

"We've got to get out of here. When the dam breaks, they'll both drown, it's as simple as that!"

It was Owen. Amy whimpered and I whispered for her to crawl to me. Then I heard another voice, familiar. "Why are you the only one who couldn't handle his bitch?" Steven.

There was no way to stop the canoe, and from the sound of it, they were just behind a cluster of rocks that obscured the view upriver. I glanced at the corpse and then back at Amy. "Climb into the water and hold onto the side."

She looked between the rocks and the water, rooted to the spot. She'd tasted hope and now it was poisoning her chances of living. I glanced back to the rocks ahead. There were thin wisps of white drifting up into the sky, smoke from a campfire.

We didn't have time. I grabbed her hands. "I need you to be brave, I'll be right beside you." I didn't wait, deciding that it was better to show my daughter how to be brave. I clambered over the side as quiet as I could, feeling the depths seize my lower body as I clung to the side of the canoe.

The lapping waves against the shore hid the splash. I carefully helped Amy into the water, clinging with just one hand to the side, just enough to keep my balance.

"Keep your head low, just enough to breathe, that's it…"

Amy's hair spread out like brown mud in the water. My memories must've faded in the nine years that my daughter had been separated from me. I distinctly recalled her red hair.

"Hey, look!" Owen had spotted us. I didn't dare sneak a peek. I kept my nose just above water, hoping that the spot I'd picked wouldn't reveal my own hair trailing behind me.

Steven was quick to dismiss my husband. "Another fucking camper body. Look at that shit, bastard got caught in his rope."

"Should we haul him out? She could be hiding inside it," Owen asked, and I heard a thud and a splash. He'd thrown a rock.

I heard Steven laugh. "Sophie would already be swimming away, or screaming. Remember the past nine years? She's done nothing but pout. After this is over, you're in the clear."

In days that seemed like another life, his words might have made me angry, but as it stood, I no longer cared. All I cared about was floating in front of me, Steven and Owen were just obstacles to that.

RIVERS OF MERCY

Amy's eyes were wide and small bubbles formed around her nose. I pressed a hand to her chest and felt her heart beating like a running rabbit. My hand pulled just enough to turn the boat, obstructing their view until we had made it around the bend and out of sight.

I didn't dare breathe. I couldn't tell how far away from them we were, or what the water could hide. *They have to have a way out, there must be a way out.*

Maybe they had a car, or a boat with a motor, a damn helicopter for all I knew, something that could take us out of this green hell and back home. I kicked my legs, slow, barely moving so I wouldn't splash and alert the two behind us until we were hidden in the trees.

I felt something slip between my feet; it might've been fish or debris, or another corpse making its way downriver. In my imagination, I saw a hand, small and delicate as it had been on the day she was taken from me, reaching up from the depths to grasp at me.

Then I looked at the face of my new daughter, the one that the universe had seen fit to send back to me, and my feet found soft gravel underneath me. We'd drifted close enough to the ad hoc shore. I tried to make as little sound as possible getting out of the river, inching my way through the gravel and piled sticks until I'd left the water.

I made sure that Amy mimicked my motions, and then I sat her on the edge of the canoe and stared into the green eyes that had once been blue. "Stay here. I have to make sure we're safe. I love you so much."

Her hand grasped at mine, causing me to pause. "What if you don't come back?"

I crouched and pulled her into a hug. "I'll come back."

She didn't believe me and I didn't blame her. I barely believed myself.

Picking her up, I sat her inside the canoe and pointed at the river. "If I'm not back in an hour, just push it back in and lay down. Someone will find you."

She didn't accept it. "Why can't you come with me?"

Another hug. "Because if Mom doesn't take care of this, then they won't stop looking for us."

This time, I ignored her small hand pulling at me and I crept into the woods, turning right when I was sure that the sounds of nature would hide my approach from the two monsters who'd shed their humanity.

My feet found water, not much, barely lapping over my ankles. The trees began to thin and once again, a light reflected off errant glass. There were a smattering of cabins, and further up, what looked like a dirt road.

Some kind of camp that had been evacuated. There were still clothes that were too fresh to have been left to nature. The water rippled, a fresh breeze disturbing the fake tranquility.

I crept to the cabin corner, craning my head to see if Steven and Owen were still there. They hadn't moved from their spot behind the rock. I quietly withdrew and ducked into the nearest cabin.

The water hadn't spared the interior. Sodden mattresses floated in every corner. I waded through it looking for something sharp or a tool, anything that I could use in my hands if I had to fight.

I had barely finished rummaging through an empty footlocker when I heard the splashing. It was soft, irregular, not footsteps at all, and was coming from the other end closer to the back entrance.

I squinted against the gloom. It looked like a section of the water was moving, the surface rising and falling in irregular rhythms. I was nearly on it before I realized it was a ball of cottonmouths.

They were mating, swirling around and barely paying me any mind. It didn't stop me from falling backwards trying to get away. I went under and heard the dim sounds of my feet kicking against the boards as I broke the surface with a huge gasp.

I felt a chill that had nothing to do with the cold mountain air. Two new voices had been added to the mountain air, shouting in alarm. They were coming.

I looked around, frantic. I had no illusions about being able to fight either of them, and there weren't a lot of places to hide. My eyes flicked to the ball of snakes and the dark water. I could hear the splashing footsteps getting closer…

The last bunk was still standing, the deteriorating mattress and pillows still in their position like they were waiting for a corpse. I lowered myself into the water, pushing against the rusted metal frame to keep myself from floating. Then I held my breath and waited.

Barely five seconds later, the door banged open and fell off the hinges in a huge splash that sent a wave rippling through the cabin interior. I felt the rough scales of a few snakes that had been disturbed by the ripples. A dark silhouette slithered over my hand, crisscrossing through the water to join its brethren.

"You fucking heard that. She's in here," Steven snarled.

He didn't give Owen a chance to respond before I heard the shot. Wood splintered and a new shaft of light shone through the roof.

"Get your ass out here, Sophie. I'll make it quick. If not, we're going to work on you just like I worked on Liz. Fucking bitch." He was a caveman beating his chest because he wanted a new toy to break, to destroy. Owen tried a softer approach.

"Babe, ignore him. I'm sorry for what happened. I-I've had all night to think about it. I'll keep you safe… really, sweetie, come out!" His voice had the same cadence as a kid promising not to lie and laughing through his teeth.

They moved deeper into the cabin while, at the same time, that long and droning horn sounded again, sonorous and insistent. The water thrummed from its vibration and then it fell silent.

I felt the water wash over me and saw them move past me, their shadows like some dangerous creature on the hunt.

Steven began to speak. "You hear that, Sophie? You're going to die if you don't come with us. The fucking dam is giving way upriver. Leon's guys say we've only got an hour, maybe two. So unless you want to drown, get your ass ou—" I heard Steven say before I came erupting from under the bedframe like a screaming demon.

He turned, trying to aim the gun, but my hands found his chest and I shoved as hard as I could. There was a clap as he pulled the trigger, but Steven had already lost his balance and the shot went wild.

The snakes went wild as he fell on top of them.

His scream was shrill, all traces of alpha male bullshit lost in the all-consuming panic and biting reptiles. I saw the lashing serpents, the bites, the fangs sinking into his open eye.

I heard Owen screaming, and I was halfway turned before I felt his fist. There was a sharp pain, and I went stumbling, falling on my ass in the cabin corner. Owen stood over me, fists balled, face contorted by his rage like some surreal nightmare of the man I'd once loved.

"You killed him, you fucking bitch." He whispered it, his throat hoarse.

One hand cradled my face (was that my blood on his knuckles?) and the other tried to keep myself from losing my balance and drowning as the world swirled around me. It closed around something metal, something that felt familiar.

Steven must've lost his grip when he'd lost the ability to breathe, and despite my vision, Owen was close, and it was hard to miss at this range. The shot almost tore the gun from my grip. I wasn't used to firearms and knew nothing about them other than where to point it. I also knew you had to pull the trigger.

The first bullet caught him in the ribs. His hands cradled his guts and he staggered forward, hand outstretched towards me. I pulled the trigger two more times, and he toppled forward.

There were minnows already nipping at the ragged bits of flesh around his wounds.

My husband's corpse… *my husband's corpse…*

WILE E. YOUNG

In another life, I would have grieved.

Exhausted, I staggered to my feet, listening to the water run off me as the snake hisses slowly died, their dance of life continuing on Steven's chest. I could hear his rasping breaths as his windpipe began to close. His one good eye stared at me, tears streaming...

The other was the size of a baseball, ugly browns and yellows running through the poisoned sclera. I think he wanted me to shoot him, but I left him to his death and the snakes that would deliver it. I heard him stop breathing as I waded back into the sun.

They'd left a radio and some food on their stand of rock, Slim Jims mostly. The radio was squalling and I heard Trevon's voice crackling through the speaker. "Guys, come in. What the fuck is happening?" I turned it off. Let them come and find the bodies floating in the cabin.

The droning horn sounded again. They were coming closer together, a warning that time was short. We wouldn't make it just floating in a scavenged canoe, but I didn't think that Steven and Owen would have been left on their own without a means to save themselves.

That thought was rewarded when I saw the small boat, motor ready and waiting. I waded through the water and clambered on, setting the gun and the food in the floorboards as I pulled the throttle. The engine cranked to life with a small cough, a black plume of exhaust drifting up into the air as I angled the boat out of the flooded campground and right back into the main river.

When I made it around the bend, I saw that the canoe was still there and called to my daughter. "Amy!"

154

She poked her head up from behind the canoe and I saw her eyes begin to fill with tears as she plunged into the river and I wrapped her up in my embrace. We may have stayed that way forever if not for the drone of the weakened dam, loud and insistent.

I could almost imagine it as words: *Stay and die.*

"Ok, Amy. I found some food, it's on the seat behind you. You eat on that while I get us home," I said, hopping out of the boat and pushing us towards deeper water.

Once again we were making our way downriver, as fast as the boat could carry us.

Amy didn't wait to eat. To a hungry kid, a few Slim Jims might as well have been a feast worthy of a king. I hadn't asked her to share.

We watched the trees pass. There were no banks. I looked for a road or trail that would take us back to civilization, but didn't see anything but the impenetrable green.

Amy finished pushing the wrapping into the boat's bed, and then she just looked at me, dark hair that had once been red, and green eyes that had once been blue watching me.

I smiled at her, and she smiled back. It was a different image than what I'd imagined, but she was just a little girl when she'd left. Now there was this pre-teen, and I heard her beautiful voice speak hesitantly. "My name isn't Amy."

My smile didn't slip, but my heart dropped. "Of course it is."

She shook her head. "My name is Layla, I'm from Little Rock. I don't—"

I reached across and despite her flinch, grabbed her hand. "You were taken from outside our house in Paris. You're from Texas. I know it was a long time ago, but whatever they told you isn't true."

Amy's eyes filled with tears. "You're not my—"

My finger jumped and my smile was gone, replaced with worry. "I am, and that isn't going to change."

She withdrew from me. I didn't blame her; the trauma of everything, what those animals had done with her, it would take time to bring her back.

We had gone another few miles when I heard a sound like a tree branch cracking, then the water next to the boat shot upward like a rock hitting the surface. There was another crack and the cold realization that we were being shot at. I pressed down hard on the clutch and the boat shot forward. I heard a clang and saw the dented metal – a bullet had ricocheted only an inch from my hand.

There were shouts along the shore and I thought I saw headlights in the trees to my right. I was bent over at my chest, breathing hard, trying not to panic. The pistol was in easy reach and the temptation was there to just pick it up and go out fighting.

You're already fighting. No use being stupid about it.

Amy was huddled in the bottom of the boat amidst the detritus of Slim Jim wrappers and cigarette butts. Her eyes were clenched tight, and she flinched at every new shot.

I didn't know what they were using, only that it wasn't shooting that fast, and as I angled us to the other side of the river the gunfire slacked off. I heard shouts from behind us, and a horn honking. It was overshadowed by another blast of warning from the distant dam.

Trucks were moving through the woods now; I could hear the tires and engines struggling on what must have been old trails. I didn't know where they were going. With my unoccupied hand, I picked up the pistol, hoping that it still had enough bullets to mean something.

The river twisted again, and the bits of foam and floating vegetation began to speed up. The current was getting stronger. I eased up on the throttle, listening.

I didn't have to wait long before we rounded the bend and I saw the high-water bridge. The debris from the flooding were clumped around the struts, wood piled high in sharp peaks that seemed to create a dam of forbidding edifices. And standing on the bridge itself were half a dozen men, rifles aimed straight and true.

The leader, Leon, stood in the center, still wearing the same rain jacket he'd been wearing last night. There was no running, not this time. I'd catch a bullet in the time it took to swing the boat back around.

Leon took his hands from his pockets. "Don't bother. Why don't you just pull that little skiff over to shore?"

I was an animal caught in a trap, steel jaws around my soul. Desperately, I looked around for an escape, some path I hadn't seen, a tributary leading out of insanity. There was only one option I could see that would get us out of this mess. I looked at the deep water. We'd have to pitch ourselves into it, let the current take us. And drown.

A bullet or a long, deep breath of water. There wasn't a choice.

My eyes flicked to the pistol next to me, solidifying my desires, and my decision to play for time. Amy wasn't going back, and I refused to be debased in some dark basement until I was all used up.

I pulled the boat to the shore and I heard Amy begin to wail, curling into a ball and quivering. My scarred heart broke all over again. I reached down and wrapped her up, listening to the footsteps racing across the bridge.

"Mom, has you. From here to eternity, mom has you."

I felt the trigger, the weight of it heavy, and I heard the men shouting for me to drop it.

"I love you so much," I whispered and jerked.

The shot was covered by the faltering damn's long and mournful drone, but I heard the clang of metal, and the tapping as the small pool of water around my feet turned a muddy red.

I glanced up and saw the men pointing their own weapons, barking their orders like dogs. My hand drifted up, the pistol held limp, and I looked at the crumpled and lifeless body of my daughter.

In my imagination, I'd always seen the trip to eternity as white light. All encompassing, warm, the things you regretted left behind, all the evil and cruelty having passed away…

Instead, I heard the click of an empty chamber and found myself still tethered to the mortal coil and in the hands of my enemies.

I didn't resist when they took me from the boat, the empty pistol taken from my hand. There was a fist, but I barely felt the pain. Tears streamed down my face as I stared at the tiny, crumpled figure on the boat floor. Then I was halfway up the embankment, and she was gone into the embrace of the river.

From far away, there was a cracking, a boom like thunder, and then a silence, like the world was holding its breath. Flocks of distant birds took to the air, but the men around me didn't seem to understand... But I did... I knew... I welcomed it.

Between the two trucks on the bridge, there was a van, and Liz was inside it. She wiggled and made guttural sobbing noises, the stump of her tongue wagging like a worm writhing on the end of a hook. There was a bandage wrapped around her head, two dark circles of blood staining the fabric through and streaming down her cheeks. They'd cut off her hands and feet, and the burned stumps wiggled like she was still trying to run.

The man himself stood next to Leon, hands thrust in his pockets and staring at me impassively until the moment they dropped me in front of him and I felt his hand strike me.

"Where's Steven and Owen!?"

I laughed in his face and felt a cold sense of satisfaction seeing that his only recourse was to hit me again.

Leon caught his hand. "Easy, I don't need a girl with a fucked-up face. I've already got that."

Trevon breathed hard and then spit in my face. I felt the fat glob of saliva roll down my cheek as he went and stood by the van, reaching out and playing with Liz' breasts as she bucked and screamed at the touch.

Leon leaned down, smiling warmly like he was talking to a favorite pet. "You ladies did a number on those fellas, let me tell you. I don't think I've ever seen such aggressive shit. Usually comes from weak assholes who feel emasculated." He looked over at Trevon again. "Well, maybe I'm spot on about that."

I don't know what he wanted from me. A conversation? Absolution? Commiseration that he was surrounded by idiots?

None of it mattered, and I watched the water under the bridge surge, sucking the debris through the trestles until there was no empty space left.

"Didn't think you had it in you to kill a kid," he said. "Hefty chunk out of my bottom line, but I'm sure you can make up for it."

I finally met his gaze. "She was my daughter."

He looked confused. "We sold your daughter a few years back. Sick fucks pay premium for kids. We don't keep a record. So you just shot some poor—"

I was on my feet, trying to dig my nails into his eyes. "SHE WAS MY—"

One punch and I was back on the concrete, and through the haze I heard his muttering. But I could also see upriver and hear the rumbling like a distant storm. Leon looked at the water rushing under the bridge, getting faster, waves splashing over the railing, and he circled his hand. "Pack it up!"

"It's too late!" I shouted. "There's nowhere to go! No horn! It's coming and you're going to fucking die!"

You could see maybe a mile upriver, the black water and overcast day shrouding the valley. But where before it had been just a distant thunder, now it was the sound of a tempest, the sound of drums. The wrath of water.

It spilled around the corner, a wave of water five stories tall, slamming against the valley walls and ripping trees from their place, joining them in the torrent bearing down on us.

The men dropped me, screaming, and I heard engines rumble as they desperately tried to escape what was coming.

I stood and saw Trevon trying to scramble into the van, and I sprinted as fast as I could. I was hurt, everything in me wanting to give up, and I wasn't as fast as I could have been. But my hands still wrapped around the back of his shirt, and I threw him to the pavement. He cracked his head, a wound that probably would have killed him in the long run. He rolled around like a newborn, yelling for the van not to leave him and crying when he saw the spinning wheels that spit gravel over the both of us.

I crouched over him, his cracked skull making him weak, and twisted his head so that he could see the flood. I saw the taillights of the trucks racing up the jeep trail a quarter mile away, heading into the flood, trying to beat it to higher ground.

WILE E. YOUNG

I imagined Leon's scream when they were wrenched from the trail, highlighted against the brown and white deluge and swallowed end over end into the maelstrom.

Trevon was crying, blubbering for forgiveness, but I could barely hear him over the crashing cascades. I laughed long and hard, relieved to see my daughter again soon.

"I'm coming to get you, baby!" I shouted.

The tidal wave reached the bridge and I closed my eyes.

ACKNOWLEDGEMENTS

WESLEY:
First and foremost, I want to thank you the reader for your constant support of my work. Without you, I would not be able to do what I love to do, and for that I thank you. Words cannot begin to describe how much I appreciate each and every one of you.

Much love and respect to Katie and Nolan, Mom, Dad, Sis, my in-laws, Joseph Hunt and family, Mary SanGiovanni, Brian Keene, Mike Lombardo, Somer and Jessie Canon, Wile E. Young and Emily Rice, Chris Enterline, Kristopher Triana, Stephen Kozeniewski, Kenzie Jennings, John Wayne Comunale, Lucas Mangum, and John Boden.

Major props to Lisa Lee Tone, Tod Clark, Kyle Lybeck, and Jamie La Chance for their editorial help and opinions. Couldn't have done this without you all.

WILE E.:
Thanks to my mentors, friends, and peers who believed and helped make this possible: Brian Keene, Stephen Kozeniewski, Lucas Mangum, Kenzie Jennings, Mary SanGiovanni, Bob Ford, Somer Canon, Kristopher Triana, Dan Volpe, Aron Beauregard, John Wayne Comunale, and a long list of others I admire.

Special thanks to my departed friends, Dallas Mayr and Jay Wilburn, for advice and time I've never forgotten.

Thank you to my wife, Emily, who has stayed with me through the worst and has ridden with me through the best, has labored over and beta-read everything, and who has helpfully told me when I needed a good kick in the pants.

BOTH AUTHORS:
We would like to thank artist Justicia Satria for the wonderful artwork and capturing exactly what we were looking for.

And Scott Cole for his hard work on making our book look amazing once again. You're the best!

WESLEY SOUTHARD is the two-time Splatter-punk Award-Winning and Imadjinn Award-Winning author of *The Betrayed*, *Closing Costs*, *One for the Road*, *Resisting Madness*, *Slaves to Gravity*, *Cruel Summer*, *Where the Devil Waits*, *The Final Gate*, *Try Again*, *They Mostly Come at Night*, and *Disasterpieces* as well as numerous short stories in various markets. Several of his works have also been translated into Italian and Spanish. He is a graduate of the Atlanta Institute of Music and he currently lives in South Central Pennsylvania with his wife and son. Visit him online at www.wesleysouthardhorror.com.

WILE E. YOUNG is from Texas, where he grew up surrounded by stories of ghosts and monsters. During his career he has managed to both have a price put on his head and win the 2021 Splatterpunk Award for Best Novel. He obtained his bachelor's degree in History, which provided no advantage or benefit during his years as an aviation specialist and I.T. guru.

9 798987 371336